MONSTER BONES

MONSTER BONES

Edited by
Stephanie Ellis
and Noel Osualdini

Cemetery Dance Publications
Baltimore
2025

Monster Bones

All stories are original to this anthology, except the following, used with permission:
Midnight Mass by F. Paul Wilson
The Companion by Joe R Lansdale, Kasey Jo Lansdale and Keith Lansdale

Cemetery Dance Publications
132B Industry Lane, Unit #7
Forest Hill, MD 21050
www.cemeterydance.com

Edited by Stephanie Ellis and Noel Osualdini
Cover artwork by Luke Spooner
Cover layout, Interior, and Ebook Design: Steven Pajak

Trade Paperback
ISBN: 978-1-964780-24-5

Contents

Slavic Folklore
Rusalka
Almost always female
Eyes glow with Green Fire

RUSALKA

Gwendolyn Kiste

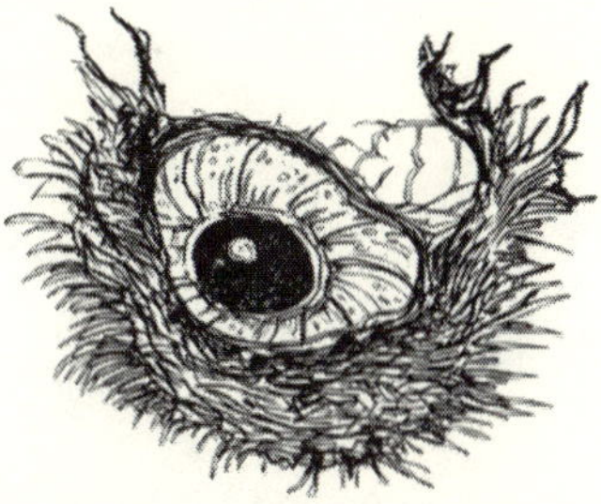

The creature I call my mother is waiting for me in the dark again.

She's tucked away in the back of the house, fully clothed and splashing in grimy bathwater.

"Little one," she hollers. "Can you hear me?"

Little one. That's been my nickname for years, even though I'm not so little anymore. I'm a grown woman now. A so-called adult.

I don't answer her. I don't even walk down the hallway. It doesn't matter. She knows I'm here anyhow. And so does he, the man who's no more than a shadow in the kitchen doorway.

"You should talk to your mother," he hisses from the gloom.

I didn't know he was watching me. He edges forward, that round face of his glistening in the moonlight. He's the closest thing I'll ever have to a father. That's of course not saying much.

I shrink back a step, not answering either one of them, not even when she calls out to me again.

"Little one, please," she says, her words burbling beneath the water.

I should scream. I should fight. I should do something, *anything* to make this stop. Instead, I run from the house, and, for tonight at least, I don't look back.

The next morning, I can barely keep my eyes open at work.

"You all right?" my coworker Felicity asks me, and I just nod and wave her off.

But she's not so easily deterred. "You want a coffee? I'll get one for both of us at the place next door."

And with that, she's gone, not even waiting for a response. I watch her leave, the swing of her hips, that long red hair flowing down her back. She's shining inside and out in ways I can't imagine. That's because I'm practically a shadow in my own life.

Everything in me is divided in two: between the reality out and about in the world, and the reality when I'm with those things I call my family.

It's funny in a way. I haven't lived in that place with my parents for a long time. Almost two decades now. But sometimes it feels like I never left. It doesn't help that I visit far too often. But that's what a good daughter is supposed to do, isn't it?

Felicity brings me the coffee like she promised, but it doesn't help. I sleepwalk through the rest of the day, fucking up an Excel spreadsheet three times because I'm too tired to see straight.

"We need you to do better than this, Bella," my boss tells me, and she doesn't even say it in a condescending tone. It's almost as if she's worried about me too.

That weekend, I return to my parents' house. I don't even know why I go there. Maybe because I'm trying to fix something. Or trying to end something.

When I walk in the door, the man who masquerades as my father is already slumped back in the green La-Z-Boy chair, the cushion molding around his body.

"You hurt your mother's feelings the other day," he says, because it's the only thing he cares about. *Her* feelings. Not mine, not his, not anyone else's. He's no more than her lackey, a cross between Renfield and Squeaky Fromme, everything in him crumbling to dust in front of my eyes.

But I can never quite hate him. He's the only person who seemed to give a damn about me when I was a kid. He would take me out for ice cream, the two of us sitting at the city park, the butter-yellow sun beating down on us, as we laughed together. When I was young, I used to think he honestly liked me. When I was grown, I realized he only liked me so long as I was quiet. So long as I was compliant.

"You've got to try harder," he would say. "We both have to try harder to make her happy."

I give him a gap-toothed grin, a smear of ice cream on my chin. "I'll do my best," I'd say, but it turns out my best was never enough for them. Especially when she got hungry, that insatiable appetite searing through her, burning a hole right into the middle of our lives.

"That's your mother," he would tell me anytime I cowered from her.

Sometimes, I'm not convinced that I belong to them. I could be the lost child of one of her victims, a kid they adopted because it was convenient. That's what I tell myself anyhow. It's easier to believe this tragedy isn't my own.

Tonight, I linger in the living room, listening for her. In the bathroom, she's still splashing in that same grimy water.

"Rusalka," I murmur. That's what she is. My mother is more spirit than woman.

She can't exist outside of water. That's the rule. But the rivers in these backwoods have become gray and polluted. That means she can't swim in the darkness like she used to. Now she's relegated to the confines of our bathtub, her skin pruning in the well water that always tastes like brine.

Our whole lives have revolved around her and her secrets. I grew up in this dubious house, not making many friends, not talking to anyone if I could help it.

"Are you okay, Bella?" my teachers would ask, and I would always force a smile.

But by the time I got to high school, all I wanted was to be normal. Naturally, it didn't work out. My mother could charm anyone I brought through the door. They didn't even ask why she always had her feet in a tub of water. They'd just gather around her, that magnetic pull always brimming in her veins.

"Sweetheart, what do you need?" she'd ask them, all while only worrying about what she needed. That's how my friends became her friends until they became nothing at all. She could devour you whole in the blink of an eye, absorbing everything you are. I would try to warn them. I would even scream. Nobody ever listened.

Nobody noticed they were missing either. They weren't the type of kids the world cared about.

"Runaways," the locals always said, and since my mother only took one every year or so, it never drew much attention.

After a while, I stopped making friends altogether. It was safer for everyone that way.

"Let's go out tonight," Felicity says to me one afternoon, and because I can't think of an excuse quick enough, I simply tell her yes.

We sit together in a back booth at an Italian restaurant, and the evening is almost halfway over before my stomach flips, and I realize this is a date. I'm on a date with the gorgeous girl from work.

"Do you have family in the area?" she asks.

I shrug. "I guess so."

She tilts her head, a small grin blossoming on her lips. "You guess so?"

I won't look at her now. "I don't see them very often," I lie.

She leans closer, her hand suddenly touching mine. "You know," she says, "you don't have to see them at all. There's no rule about it."

I gape at her, confusion blurring my vision. "That's not true," I whisper. "I owe them something."

I'm just not sure what that something is.

Afterward, I drive out of town to the little one-story house nestled back in the woods. My mother is awake. She's always up and restless in the dark. The curtains are pushed back on the nearby window, and her body shimmers in the moonlight, her wild hair falling in every direction, her clothes almost threadbare. She's not quite living, and she's not quite dead. She's something in between.

I've barely walked through the bathroom door before she perks up.

"You were with somebody tonight, weren't you?" she asks.

A chill rushes through me. "No," I say, but she already knows the truth.

"Her scent's like peppermint." My mother smirks at me. "You should bring her around. I'd love to meet her."

I back into the hall, not breathing, not blinking. The man who might be my father is still in the recliner in the living room, eavesdropping on our conversation.

"She has no right," I whisper, but he only exhales a sharp laugh.

"That's your mother. She's got a right to anything she wants." He turns to me, his gaze gone dark. "Besides, we didn't raise you to be greedy."

"It's not greedy to want your own life." I grit my teeth. "Besides, she's already taken everyone else from me."

My father waves me off. "She says that's not true. She told me your friends just ran off."

I roll my eyes. "You know that's not what happened."

He sneers at me. "There are two sides to every story."

"Yes," I say. "There's the truth and her lies. That's two sides, isn't it?"

On Friday, Felicity asks me out again. This time, I don't hesitate.

"Yes," I say, beaming.

She takes me to dinner, a red tablecloth kind of place that's way too fancy for someone like me. All evening, she chatters on about her own family, the potluck kind where people smile at each other and genuinely mean it.

"That sounds nice," I say, my heart squeezing in my chest every time she laughs.

We close out the place, the lights flickering off overhead, one by one. We head outside together.

"Thanks for a lovely evening," she says, and kisses me goodnight. My skin buzzes, as I watch her walk across the parking lot, that red hair like a forest fire.

She turns back at the last moment. "You're wrong, you know," she says.

I stare at her, dread churning in me. "Wrong?" I ask. "About what?"

"Your family," she says. "You don't owe them a damn thing."

As she climbs into her car and pulls away, I wave goodbye, her words roiling in me.

"She belongs to me," my mother whispers when I visit the next day. "Everything of yours is mine too."

"We didn't raise you to be greedy," my father says again, and he keeps saying it until I walk out the door.

The days with Felicity bleed into months, and she's suddenly everywhere in my life. The two of us antiquing on weekends, splitting a pitcher of mimosas at brunch, learning new recipes from YouTube. Her smile shifts my world, a future in the making.

"We could move in together," she whispers to me in bed, the two of us curled up in her apartment. "We could move anywhere."

"But I can't leave," I say, even though I don't know why.

The next day, I return to my family. Like always, my mother sleeps all day in the water, her strange snoring vibrating through the walls. Meanwhile, the man who's probably my father sits with me in the living room. We play Yahtzee three times before lunch and spend the afternoon watching old episodes of *Columbo*.

He keeps his eyes trained on the television. "If you don't want to share," he says to me, "then maybe you should just stay with us. There's nothing good out in the world anyhow."

"Nothing good," I repeat, my body sprawled out on the couch, everything in me going numb.

I don't return to work. I don't call off either. With my mother's voice lilting on the air, I sink into this house, barely moving for days.

My father makes us hot dogs for lunch every day, and I pretend to enjoy it.

It's more than a week, maybe more than two weeks, before there's a knock on the door. When I answer, Felicity is standing on the other side.

I gape at her. "What are you doing?"

"I was worried about you," she says, her face gray. "We were all worried."

"I'm fine," I say, and fidget in the doorway. "How did you find me?"

"There was talk that your family lived out here." She glances around at the odd wooded landscape. "There aren't many houses besides this one."

"You can't be here," I start to say, but my father is right behind me, a bright grin on his face.

"Come in," he says, and Felicity does as he requests.

"Please, don't." I tug on her arm. "You don't understand."

But my father is already guiding her down the hallway. "Right this way," he says. He leads her into the bathroom and then he leaves us alone. He never admits what my mother does to people. And he certainly never watches.

My mother is bobbing in the water, everything about her looking like a curse. "Finally," she says. "I've been waiting to meet your friend, Bella."

Next to me, Felicity is staring at my mother, her jaw slack. "What *are* you?" she wheezes, but there's no answer in the world that will suffice.

I seize up in the doorway, my life on repeat. This is what's always happened, all my hopes and dreams dissolving around me. My mother gets what my mother wants. And of course she wants the same thing that I do. I'm her kin. I never wanted to admit it to myself, but I know it's true: I'm my parents' daughter.

But that doesn't mean I have to end up just like them.

My mother is reaching for Felicity, but I won't let her do this again. I rush forward, shoving the creature back into the water.

"Run," I say, and Felicity doesn't hesitate. She's out the door in a flash, crashing through the living room and onto the porch.

"Have a nice night," my father says from the other room, because he'd rather be oblivious than actually open his eyes.

But my eyes are wide open, and I'm looking right at my mother. And she's glaring back at me.

"You're nothing but a spoiled brat," she seethes, spit spewing from the corners of her mouth.

I can't help but grin at her. "That's better than being you," I say.

She's ready to do the one thing we both know she's wanted since I was too young to stand. Her mouth unhinges, and she lunges at me, but I'm quicker than her. I dive toward the water, yanking out the plug and tossing it against the far wall.

She lets out a wail that splits the sky, as she scrambles for the faucet, desperate to flip it on, but I knock her backward. The drain is faster than I expect. When it's done, there's nothing left but a desiccated form in the shape of a monster. In the shape of my mother.

My father staggers in, a moment too late. He falls to his knees, cradling what's left of her. "All you had to do was share," he says to me. "Why couldn't you do that, Bella?"

He forgets that's all I ever did. I shared things with my mother that she had no right to take. Never again.

I push past him, slipping into the hallway. My father is screaming and stammering and sobbing behind me, his voice like rusted nails against my back, and part of me wants to comfort him, to stay with him now that she's gone. But I already know that I can't do that. This place could still devour me whole. So I just keep on walking, until the door slams, and he fades out like a forgotten dream, everything fading out.

Outside, Felicity is waiting for me, her face pallid, her body still shaking. "You all right?" she asks, and as she reaches out to take my hand, all I can do is toss back my head and exhale the brightest laugh in the world, drowning out everything and everyone that came before.

It sounds a little like madness. It sounds a little like freedom too.

YOU'RE BACK

David Wellington

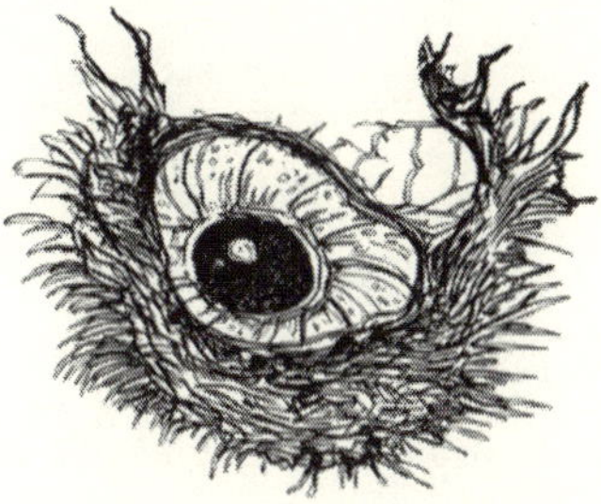

You wake up, stiff and achy, chilly. Maybe because you're barefoot, even though you're wearing a three-piece suit. You can't remember a thing about what happened or how you got here. Must have been a hell of a night—

Oof. That smell. Chemicals, or something. In the dark it's hard to tell where the smell is coming from. You stumble to the door, and it's locked, chained. It takes you way too long to remember the key is in your jacket pocket. You reach through the iron bars and turn the key and you're out, you're free.

Outside there's a moon shining on you. You and a hundred gravestones. Crosses. Obelisks, laid out with no pattern. Winding little paths run this way and that. Big marble and granite stones with names and dates and simpering little mottos. I KNOW MY REDEEMER LIVETH.

A … a graveyard? They put you in the graveyard?

You must be dead.

But then how are you still up and moving?
Sadly, this is not just a sick joke.
There's something you need to do.

Light and warmth behind a familiar window. The sound of gentle laughter. It's almost too much to bear. You touch the glass with fingers that hardly bend. The people in there won't understand. You should go. You start to turn away, but—no.

You have a funny feeling. A prickle at the back of your neck that you can never resist. You're supposed to be here. You reach again and tap at the glass. *Tap*. When the people inside look up, you give them a cheery wave.

That's when the screaming starts. But she—she doesn't scream.

She's wearing black. Alone among them, she hasn't forgotten you. And when she looks up, she meets your eyes, and she knows. She knows who you are.

The others come out and drive you away. They shout and one of them throws rocks at you, his tie swinging, his face red and wet. They don't want you here.

You go. What choice do you have? But you glance back, just once.

She's still there. Watching you walk away.

Later …

You didn't know what else to do except wander around. Trying to remember. Then you staggered out into the street and you heard a car horn and squealing brakes and … and … something happened.

You don't think you meant to do it.

But now the idiot is just lying there, looking off to one side. His neck looks wrong. The skin's all bunched up and his jaw is loose inside its sack of skin. His girlfriend is still inside the car and she's screaming, her gloved hands flying up to clutch at the sides of her beehive hairdo.

Idiot in a letterman jacket just had to be a hero.

"C'mon, buddy. C'mon. Get up," you tell him, because it should be that easy. If they let you out, surely anybody can come back if they want to. "You're scaring her."

He doesn't move. You sigh and shamble away. You've got something to do.

You wish you could remember what.

Later still. The first ray of the sun comes crawling down the street. You've been looking forward to it. Anything to warm up this old, cold world. Except where the light touches you, it feels wrong. You're not supposed to be up and walking during the day. Your neck itches and you turn around. You have to get back to your crypt.

There's still time. Just.

You can reach the graveyard if you hurry. Maybe your knees are in lousy shape but you can make it. Slink back inside. Reach through the bars and lock yourself back in. Knock the dirt off your feet, lie down, cross your arms across your chest. Put things back the way they were.

You got one night off from being dead. You didn't exactly make the most of it.

Oh, well.

Dark. Nobody knows what darkness is really like, not when they're alive.

No light.

No eyes to see it if there was.

Nothing smells, nothing hurts, nothing soothes you.

You start to sink. It doesn't feel like drowning, no, nor being enveloped by quicksand. It just feels like you're being absorbed. Dissolved, but not in a bad way. It feels like maybe this is over, and that, brother, is a relief. In a second this will all be over and you won't be responsible, you won't be bothered by what you did or didn't do. What you coudn't fix. Who could ask for anything more?

Well, maybe angelic choirs and a big cheeseburger and getting to see Gramps again would be nice.

But this is pretty good, too.

Sink.

Let go.

If only your neck would stop itching.

You wake up, stiff and achy, chilly. You can't remember a thing about what happened or how you got here. Must have been a hell of a night—

There's a faint smell. Chemicals, or something. Door's locked. You reach through the iron bars and turn the key and you're out, you're free.

Why can't you remember anything? Weird.

Outside there's a moon shining on you. You and a hundred or so gravestones. Crosses. Urns. Little square stones with names and dates and simpering mottos. I KNOW MY REDEEMER LIVETH.

A … a graveyard? They put you in the graveyard?

This is not just a sick joke.

There's something you need to do.

You walk for a long time. You're not sure where you're going. The back of your neck itches like hell and you keep scratching but it doesn't help.

You just want to walk and figure out where you're supposed to go. Is that so wrong? But then there's a complication. You're not exactly sure what happened. You hear car horns and headlights pin you up against a wall. Then there's a cop in a peaked cap and he pulls out a revolver and things get—

Messy.

You look down at your hands and they're red.

Wasn't supposed to happen like that.

In the distance: sirens. You get moving, you try to run, but the lights are right behind you.

Up ahead there's something you almost recognize. A house. A

house where there's light and warmth behind the windows, oh, God, warmth, and gentle laughter and—and—*her*—

You never reach it. Bullets tear through your legs, your back. You start to crawl. Bits of you get left behind but who cares. Even if you're just a stain on the street that itch is still with you, still driving you on. Something touches the back of your neck.

It's a cop's heavy leather-soled shoe. Pinning you in place.

"Our Father, who art in Heaven," he whispers. Is he crying?

You got one night off from being dead. You didn't exactly make the most of it.

Oh, well.

Gunshots. One, two, three in your skull. Even that's not enough, you think it'll take a lot more than—

The cops take a second to reload.

"Thy Kingdom come."

Bang.

Dark. Nobody knows what darkness is really like, not when they're alive.

No light.

No eyes to see it if there was.

Nothing smells, nothing hurts, nothing soothes you.

You start to sink. In a second this will all be over. Who could ask for anything more?

Well, maybe coming back as a bird would be nice. You'd like to know what it feels like to fly, to just flap your wings and fly.

But this is pretty good too.

Sink.

Let go.

If only your neck would stop itching.

You wake up, stiff and achy, chilly. Must have been a hell of a night.

Door's locked. Turn they key and you're out, you're free.

Why can't you remember anything? Why?

The moon and a couple hundred gravestones. A couple vaults, like yours, but not many. Mostly little square stones with names and dates and simpering mottos. I KNOW MY REDEEMER LIVETH.

A … a graveyard? They put you in the graveyard?

There's something you need to do.

Light and warmth behind a familiar window. The sound of gentle laughter. It's almost too much to bear. You touch the glass with fingertips like claws. They won't understand. You start to turn away, but—no.

You have a funny feeling. That prickle at the back of your neck that you can never resist. You're supposed to be here. You reach again and scratch at the glass. *Skritch skritch*. When the people inside look up, you give them a cheery wave.

That's when the screaming starts. But *she—she* doesn't scream.

She stands up. You can tell *she*'s scared but *she* doesn't want to show it. *She* walks over to the glass. Puts *her* hand up against it, mirroring yours. *She* even tries to smile for you.

And that is so good. That feels so right.

But it's not enough.

You need something from *her*. The itch at the back of your neck is driving you crazy. If *she* would just give you want you want.

Damn *she*'s pretty. Just like always.

Wait—have you done this before?

How many times?

The itch at the back of your neck tells you it doesn't matter. Focus on her. *Her* hair—it was darker before, you think. Less gray. And maybe the skin around *her* eyes was a little smoother. But it's *her*, definitely, the one you came to find.

She can forgive you, and let you go.

But *she* has to say it.

The itch is about ninety per cent of all you are, now. You open your mouth. You're going to ask *her* to say the words, and then—

Except you forgot one thing.

You don't have a tongue. Not anymore. It fell out on the way over here.

She's crying. *She* seems to understand you want something, but *she* can't tell what. It's a damned shame. I wish you could tell *her,* pal. Then we could stop doing this.

You got one night off from being dead. You tried so damned hard to make the most of it.

The sun will be up soon.

You'll have to come back.

You wake up, stiff and achy, chilly. You can't remember a thing.

Door's locked. There's a key … and you're out, you're free.

Why can't you remember anything? God damn it. Not a thing.

The moon and a couple hundred gravestones. A bunch of vaults, like yours. A little village of the dead. The hill is covered in little square stones with names and dates.

A … a graveyard? They put you in the graveyard?

A sick joke. It really is.

There's something you need to do.

Only you can't remember.

You walk for a long time. You're not sure where you're going. The back of your neck itches like hell and you keep scratching but it doesn't help. Even when the skin comes up, when you feel the bones back there. Still, that damned itch.

You just want to walk and figure out where you're supposed to go. A place with light and laughter and gentle windows. Wait, no. So hard to think, sometimes.

Her—

Mother? Wife? Just a friend?

It's so damned hard! There's cobwebs in your brain and you can't—you just can't think straight! Headlights wash over you and you hiss, except it sounds more like a gurgle. The car behind you stops and a door pops open, slams shut again.

"Mister," he says. "Hey, mister—you don't look so good."

You turn and see him there, the idiot, just standing there in his long, shaggy hair and his letterman jacket. The girl inside the car has crimped hair and she's reaching for something. A—a gun?

You stagger forward and grab at him, the idiot, and he goes down.

Why can't you remember? Your neck itches like hell and you just—can't—

The girl fires. She doesn't even roll her window down first. It explodes in a cobweb of—of brain—and—no, that's your brains, that's—

She screams and screams even when you turn to leave.

You try so hard to remember. You try to come up with a name, just something to hang a memory on. Who the hell are you?

That's when it comes to you, the best idea you've had in a long time. You stagger back to the graveyard. The itch in your neck says otherwise, it demands you turn around and—and—do something. But you're going to ignore it … tonight.

Tonight?

Have you done this before?

And that brings it back, all the times you've woken up, barefoot and chilly. All the times you've unlocked the padlock, all the time you staggered up the street. It feels like you've traveled hundreds of miles, all on broken feet.

Not once in all those nights did you—did you—

Damn the itch, the unbearable itch. So hard to think.

You have to know. You have to at least have a name. You have a name, damn it! Everybody has a name!

And when they die, they chisel that name into the stone. Into the stone above the door of their crypt.

The graveyard's full of names. Names are the graveyard's chief export. Because a name is a memory. It's the last thing you own.

You stumble up the hill. Your knees are so stiff, and the itch in the back of your neck just. Won't. Quit. Pulling you in the opposite direction. But if you can find the name, you know you can find more. More facts. The dates you were born and died. Maybe the names of some other family members. It's a place to start.

You have to know.

The itch makes you weak so you're crawling on all fours by the time you get to the crypt. You don't so much crawl to the gate as you wriggle, like a worm. Leaving bits of you behind, a trail of what you were. The name—

It takes all you've got left to look up. To tilt your head back. Only one of your eyes seems to work, now, but that's enough. You swivel it around in its socket and your mouth sags open. There's a lintel above the crypt door, a place to put a name, and there are letters chiseled into it, yes—

LOVED.

That's all it says. No name. No dates. Just LOVED.

Somebody loved you.

She loved you.

She didn't need to put your name up there to remember you by, *she*—

You start to sink. In a second this will all be over. Who could ask for anything more?

Well, you could.

Because this last moment of consciousness, it's unbearable. It's utter agony. Because you know.

You know it won't last. You'll be coming back.

Sink. Try, anyway.

Let go. As if you could.

Your neck still itches.

The boy in his stupid hooded sweatshirt grabs for you, the girl with the purple hair reaches for something in her purse it's a gun you're pretty sure it's a—

The boy goes down, his neck twisted.

The girl screams. It's not a gun, she's got something else, it's black and rectangular and shiny and she—she puts it to her ear, and—

What the hell is that? You need her help. You need her to tell you—something. You stumble forward, smash through the glass, reach for her—

No, it's not *her*. It's some other girl. It's not—

Behind you, sirens and flashing lights.

It takes you half the night to remember the key is in your jacket pocket.

You seem to remember there were nights when you never found

it. When you spent the whole night just reaching through the bars, pushing yourself against the unyielding metal, the itch telling you to try. To keep trying.

Lots of nights like that.

Tonight will be better. Reach through the bars. Work the lock.

Outside there's moonlight and a thousand or so gravestones in neat rows, marching over the side of the hill. Up here your crypt is the only one left, and the grass grows tall through cracks in the pathways. You can't read the gravestones. You know there are words there but your eyes don't work like that anymore.

Your neck itches.

Your damned neck.

It's telling you to walk. To keep walking.

It doesn't care that you don't have legs anymore.

If you focus, if you try, you can just about see. You can't feel anything, not even the surface of the road. But you can move, a little. You can sort of wriggle and crawl, leaving bits of you behind. A trail of what you were.

Cars pass by, their headlights like screams inside your empty skull. There's so little of you left now the drivers don't even see you, so you have to stay out of their way.

You're almost there.

Up ahead, light and warmth behind windows and—and gentle laughter, except—except you can't hear anything. You can't remember the last time you heard anything at all. If you really focus, if you try, you can just about see shapes and a bit of color.

You really want to see this.

You're going to make it this time.

You can just about see the windows. And behind them—*she'll* be there, behind them, *she*—

There's a sign out front, a colorful square hanging in the overgrown yard. You pull yourself forward on stumps, on bone and dry scraps of flesh, closer. Ever closer to those windows. Are those … boards? Nailed across the door?

The windows are broken. Wait. No. *She*—

If only you could—

Remember.

There's no light in there. No warmth. Not anymore. They're gone. They're all gone.

She's not there anymore.

The first ray of the sun comes crawling down the street. Where the light touches you, it feels wrong. You're not supposed to be—

You're not supposed to be.

Your neck itches.

There's still time.

You might not make it all the way to the graveyard. That's okay. As long as you keep moving, the itching is bearable. And then—you'll sink.

You'll fade.

But the itching won't stop.

You got one night off from being dead. You didn't exactly make the most of it.

Who could ask for more?

CHARNEL MOON

Ben Monroe

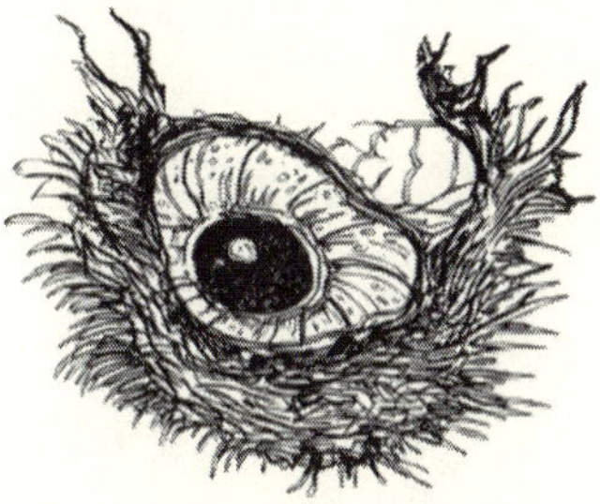

It wasn't until he was pulling rumpled bills out of his wallet that Charley Walker noticed the blood under his fingernails. He tossed a five and a couple of singles onto the counter next to a six-pack of Coors and waited patiently for his change. He saw a small paper bowl filled with shiny brown nuggets on a shelf near the cash register. The clerk had just popped a couple of them into his mouth as Charley approached with his purchase. "Whatcha eatin'?" he asked the dark-skinned man working the counter.

The clerk glanced up from a small TV, which was playing something in a language Charley didn't recognize. "Dates," he said, swallowing, then rang up the beer. "It's mid Ramadan," he added, then handed Charley his change.

Charley shrugged. "Ramadan, huh?" he said. "I thought you couldn't eat anything for that."

The man—Farid, Charley guessed from the nameplate pinned to

his shirt—stared at Charley for a moment, then forced a grin. "The month of Ramadan goes from the new moon, to the new moon of the following month," he said. "We fast during the daylight hours. When the sun goes down, we may have a light meal."

"Oh, gotcha," Charley said. "I guess it'd be kinda tough to not eat for an entire month." He pocketed his change and picked up his beer.

"Indeed," Farid replied.

Charley stepped away from the counter and walked toward the exit door. The moon rose over the horizon in the east through the window. He knew that tomorrow was the full moon, because he'd planned this trip accordingly. Charley usually tried to do his work as close to the full moon as possible. That way he had moonlight to see by and didn't have to rely on artificial light which could give him away. "Well, you're almost halfway there, I suppose," he said, gesturing to the moon through the store's front window. "Have a good Ramadan then." And he waved a half-hearted goodbye as he stepped out of the store. Farid was back to his show and didn't respond.

Charley hated small talk. But he'd learned over time that if he chatted briefly with people like Farid, they tended to forget him. If he was standoffish, or evasive, chances are they'd think about him more. Post about their weird, rude customer on Facebook or something. Remember him more than he maybe wanted. A quick, boring chat about nothing important, and chances were the guy would forget all about him.

Besides, what did he have to be nervous about? It's not like he'd murdered a guy or anything. No, the body was already dead when he dismembered it.

Charley stepped out into the night, under the fluorescent lights which illuminated the parking lot of the small gas station. Charley approached his grimy green pickup truck parked under the glow of the perimeter lamps. A quick peek into the open bed told him nobody had messed with the three large plastic coolers while he was in the store. He dropped the six-pack on the seat next to him and gunned the engine. The truck's tires spat gravel as it lurched out onto the blacktop and sped off onto the mostly empty highway.

He cracked open a beer and sucked it down while he drove north along Highway 1. The Pacific Ocean stretched off beyond the California coast to his left, the horizon lost completely, black and ominous under the night sky. Charley was driving carefully, keeping an eye out for signs of traffic and especially any cops. But the road was empty, just the occasional car speeding by across the road, going south. Nobody had been in his rearview mirror for a while.

In less than half an hour he'd finished a second beer and was slowing down as he approached the outskirts of Monterey. He signaled, slowed, and then crossed over the yellow double dividing line. Then crossed the highway and into the parking lot of the tiny boat launch he'd used to moor his boat for the last year.

He liked this place because there was no attendant. He had a key to get through the gate to the boat launch and never saw anyone else using it. Only another dozen boats docked here, and he never had to worry about anyone recognizing him.

It took Charley about fifteen minutes to drag the coolers down onto the deck of his boat, a small walkaround style fishing boat he'd christened "Tiburon." He checked his watch; the numbers glowed 7:23 p.m. He was making good time.

Soon he was speeding along the open ocean. The California coastline disappeared behind him as he arrowed straight out into the sea. During the winter time, his preferred dumping area was up near the Farallon Islands, because that's when the great whites swarmed the place. He enjoyed watching them churn the water as they disposed of his cargo. But it was early spring now, and they'd mostly vacated. He just needed to get far enough offshore that he'd be able to work undisturbed.

Once he was about five miles from shore, he killed the engine, and the Tiburon slowed until it was dead in the water. Charley let the boat drift for a few minutes, taking in the ocean's stillness. But even in early spring it was too cold to want to spend much time out here, so he got to work.

One by one he opened the coolers, exposing the grisly contents within. He'd done this enough times in the past that dumping them was quick work. He'd leverage one up onto the starboard gunwale, grab the handles at either side, and just let it tip over, blood and bits slipping out over the side of the boat into the dark water.

The first time he'd tried doing this, he'd used one large cooler big enough to hold the entire dismembered remains of a missing socialite. A socialite who'd seen too much for his client's liking. It had been heavy and awkward, and tipped backward into the boat. He'd had to dump the parts by hand then and had a hell of a time cleaning the deck when he got back to shore. So now he did it in smaller portions. *Bite-sized*, he thought, chuckling as a stream of intestine slithered out of the box into the sea with a wet, slurping noise.

As the guts disappeared below the ocean's surface, his mind wandered. Maybe this would be his last run. He'd saved up enough over the years that he could quietly disappear if he wanted to. Maybe pack up his meager belongings, empty his bank account, and drive off somewhere his clients could never track him down. He remembered once reading about a small town in West Texas so spread out that once you got out of the small downtown, you'd have to walk for miles to bump into a neighbor. Get a small house, maybe a job at the local grocery or hardware store, and just start again under a blanket of anonymity.

It took less than a quarter of an hour to dump all three coolers overboard. After closing the lid on the last one, Charley leaned over the gunwale and saw a few dark red trickles down the side of the boat. He sluiced them clean with a bucket of bleach and water. He'd have to remember to clean out the coolers later. In the past, he'd dumped them overboard too. But then he realized that going into the local Target every few months to buy new ones was an unnecessary risk and a needless expense. For as well as his clients paid for his disposal services, it wasn't worth the chance that someone might wonder.

As he stood back up, he saw the first fin break the surface of the water nearby. And then another. He hadn't counted on sharks in this spot, but they were a welcome sight. The dismembered portions of the nosy reporter he'd dumped overboard must have gotten their attention. Charley loved watching them. They were consummate predators, so perfectly adapted to their environment that they hadn't felt the need to evolve for millions of years. Truth be told, Charley was a little jealous of them.

"Eat up, fishies," he grunted as he secured the bucket in a corner of the deck, next to the empty coolers. A fin slid above the surface, followed by the sleek, pale body of a shark. The eye and mouth broke above the water, and it gaped at him. As the beast's mouth closed, Charley glimpsed a pale, white hand sliding down its gullet. And then it submerged below the water's black surface and was gone.

He pulled a burner phone out of his pocket, thumbed it until the contact number they had given him earlier appeared. Then he typed in "Done." Shortly after, his main phone pinged and he saw that the proper remuneration for the job had been delivered. He tossed the burner overboard, where it disappeared with a faint *plip!*

Charley started the Tiburon up again, gunned the engine and swung the boat around. Thoughts of freedom and escape whispered in the back of his mind. Thoughts that this would be a perfectly good way to end it. He could put this old life behind him. Start afresh somewhere else. He took one last look at this stretch of ocean he'd come to know so well. Soon he was heading back to shore. His night's work complete, and he was ready for a long, meandering drive home. One last drive down Highway 5. He thought he'd savor it.

Charley always took a different route home from his disposal jobs and planned for a couple of days on the road. It was only a few hours from the dock outside of Pescadero back to his home in the outskirts of Alcosta, but he liked to drag the return trip out a little. And it wasn't like there was anybody at home waiting for him. Besides, he didn't like his clients knowing where he was going, or how he got the work done. Mostly, they didn't ask. His process was very much of the "don't ask, don't tell" variety.

The moon was high overhead, and checking the clock on the dashboard of his truck he saw it was nearly 1:00 a.m. He could usually coast on adrenaline and caffeine for a few hours after a job, but he was about at the breaking point. Charley's eyes started drooping, and he had to shake his head frequently to stay awake on the long drive. It was time to look for a place to crash for the night.

He didn't like to use the mapping apps on his phone when he was working. He was wary of leaving a digital trail behind him if he did. So he usually just drove until he saw a roadside motel that didn't look like it had a very full parking lot. He'd been at this work for a couple of years now and had yet to stay in the same place twice.

Driving along California's Highway 5 through the central valley was an exercise in monotony. Long stretches of highway would go on for miles before seeing the lights of any cities. Late at night, with few others on the road aside from the occasional long-haul cargo truck, it was mostly just darkness.

Charley's head drooped. A moment later he felt the truck shudder and snapped his eyes open, head up. He was veering off the side of the road, the tires rumbling on the drunk bumps along the road's shoulder. He took his foot off the gas, gently pressed down on the brake, and turned the car back into its proper lane.

That was enough for him. How would he start a new life if he got himself killed by falling asleep at the wheel? He gripped the steering wheel, staring ahead along the highway, and resolved to crash at the next motel he saw, empty parking lot or not.

He drove carefully for another five miles, hands white-knuckled on the steering wheel, when he saw a blue-and-white sign on the side of the road bearing the icons for *Gas/Food/Lodging*. No city sign, though. Just one of those lonely roadside oases of civilization lost between the places where people live. Charley took the exit as soon as he saw it. The offramp curled up onto an overpass above the highway, came down on the other side, and emptied onto a frontage road. His headlights showed a long, broad stretch of empty field in front of him, one of the multitude of central valley farms.

He was at a crossroads, a T-intersection, and he cast around for some clue where to go next. To his right he saw a signpost had cracked and fallen into the roadside brush. He slowly drove the truck toward it. He let the truck idle and got out to look at the fallen sign. From how it was splayed out on the ground, he could make out that it showed if he continued to the right, he would be headed in the right direction for all his gas, food, and lodging needs.

Charley climbed back into the truck and followed the road for a few more miles as it slowly angled away from the highway. He was feeling good and lost, wondering if the sign wasn't pointing in the other direction before it had broken. Then the road veered to the left, and he saw a small motel in the distance. A glowing sign in front of the building towered above the road, making it visible from a distance. As he approached, he saw it said *Pickman's Motel,* blazing in blue neon.

Charley pressed down on the accelerator, speeding up now that he had a destination in sight. As he got closer, he was pleased to see a flashing red *Vacancy* under the motel's name. He slowed and turned into the small parking lot. There was space for maybe two dozen vehicles in the lot, but there were no other cars parked there.

"Perfect," he muttered as he pulled into a spot in front of the building, near the door marked *Office.*

Charley slumped back in his chair and rubbed his face with his hands. He still had two beers left on the seat next to him, and he cracked one open, draining it in a few gulps. He shoved the other one into his deep jacket pocket, grabbed a worn, dingy duffel bag from the back seat, and headed toward the motel's office.

An electronic chime pinged overhead when he stepped through the door into the motel office. The first thing he noticed was the cold. It was a chilly night outside, and he felt like it was almost the same temperature in the office. He zipped up his jacket and stepped toward the front desk.

The next thing that Charley noticed was the smell. The air in the small office was tinged with an incense of some sort. Not quite patchouli, but a sweet, smoky musk hung in the air. And under that, the faint smell of roasting meat. His mouth watered and he suddenly realized how hungry he was. He regretted not looking for a McDonald's or something along the way.

Charley waited a minute and then tapped on a tiny chrome desk bell twice. Just as the last chime was diminishing and he was about to slap it a third time, a door opened behind the desk, and a woman emerged.

She was tall, with long dark hair spilling down over her shoulders. Dark slacks clung tight to her legs, and she wore a burgundy sweater like it was made for her. But it was her eyes that caught Charley's attention, made his breath catch in his throat. They were dark, too, almost black. He'd never seen eyes like those before, and for a moment he couldn't look away.

"Need a room?" she said, her voice a low, smoky near-whisper. She had a thick accent he couldn't place. Maybe Middle Eastern, but he wasn't sure. It was a little like the guy who'd helped him at the convenience store earlier.

Charley practically had to shake his head to clear it. He blinked twice, then stammered, "Yeah, I need a room."

"I see," she said, and tapped the keyboard on the office computer to rouse it from sleep. "Just one night?"

He thought about that. "Let's make it two," he said. "I'm probably going to sleep in tomorrow. I mean today, I guess," he said, glancing at the clock on the wall over her head. It was almost 2 a.m. "I can take an extra day or two, I suppose. I'm taking the scenic route."

"Well, that's nice," she said, looking up at him from the keyboard. She tapped away, setting up his stay on the computer.

Charley watched her out of the corner of his eye as she registered him in the computer. He was trying to be nonchalant, pretending to stare out the large window that looked out onto the parking lot, and the road beyond.

"Hey, anywhere close still open where I could grab a bite to eat?" he asked. Whatever that smell was coming from beyond the office, it was making him hungry. His stomach growled.

She looked up and smiled, then shook her head. "Sorry, no," she said. "There's a diner another two miles up the road, but it closes at midnight."

Charley shrugged. "Ah, well. My fault for not packing a sandwich, I suppose."

She smiled, then held out her hand. "May I please see your ID?"

"Oh, sure," he said, then fumbled in his wallet for it. He had a fake ID and credit card for when he was on the road. As he handed the ID card to her, he noticed there was still a bit of dried blood under his fingernails. He'd have to scrub them clean later.

As she took the ID, she glanced down at his hands briefly, and then back up to his eyes. Then Charley noticed her leaning in slightly toward him. Her eyes were on his, and he noticed her taking a deep breath through her nose. Like she was sniffing the air around him. Smelling him.

Weird, he thought, *but okay.*

She hesitated, then put the ID card on the keyboard and began typing in his information. "I tell you what," she said as her fingers raced across the keys. "I've got some leftovers from my dinner earlier. I'll bring you a small plate. Something to hold you over until morning."

"Uh, sure, that'd be great," Charley said, his stomach grumbling again. "As long as it's no trouble."

"No trouble at all," she said, then handed him back his ID. "You're quite a way from Los Angeles. Are you coming, or going?"

He slid the card with the fake address into his wallet. "Oh, I'm on my way home." He picked up the duffel bag and slung it over his shoulder.

"But not in any rush?" she asked. "Family's not waiting for you?"

He shook his head. "No, I live alone. Not even a pet to get back to. Like I said, taking the scenic route."

She slid a scratched brass key across the countertop toward him. It hung from a dingy green plastic *Pickman's Motel* key fob. No slogan or anything, nothing about being the "best on Highway 5" or any other such trite marketing pitch. Just the address. Almost like they didn't want to be noticed.

"Room 11," she said. "Just go out the door, take a left around the corner of the building and you can't miss it."

He took the key and tucked it into his pocket. "Sounds good," he said. "Can't wait to crash. I'm dead on my feet here."

She nodded and smiled. "I'll let you settle in, then be by in a few minutes with something for you to eat."

"You sure it's no trouble?" Charley asked.

"None at all," she replied. "You're not the first person who's come in road-weary and missed dinner."

"Well, I sure appreciate it," he said. "See you soon." He adjusted his duffel bag over his shoulder, and a moment later was out the door.

Charley was splashing water on his face when he heard a light knock at the door. He toweled off as he crossed the small room, bare feet shuffling sluggishly across the thick shag carpeting. He'd pulled the blackout curtains closed when he first came in, and the single table lamp he'd turned on cast a wan, dim light.

He opened the door to see the woman standing outside, holding a plate in her hands. A thick, meat stew poured over yellow saffron-infused rice. A few rounds of sliced cucumber sprinkled with herbs to the side.

"My family recipe," she said. "I hope you like it."

Charley's mouth was already watering. He took the plate from her, the rich smell almost overwhelming him. "It smells amazing," he said. "Thanks again."

"My pleasure," she said. "Just leave the plate in front of your door when you're finished."

Charley nodded. "Hey, I never got your name," he said as she was turning to leave.

"Call me Sahira," she replied. "I'll let you eat. I have to get back to the office, anyway. My family is waiting."

"I didn't realize this was a family business," Charley replied.

"Yes," Sahira said. "My brothers and I. We took it over recently."

"That's cool," Charley said. "Kind of out of the way, but hopefully business is good."

"It's fair," she said. "There are other reasons, though. We like the location."

Charley stifled a yawn. "Well, thanks again for the dinner. It looks great."

"I think you'll like it. Like I said …"

"Old family recipe," Charley interrupted.

"Exactly," Sahira replied, then turned and walked away.

Charley watched her as she walked away, enjoying his view of the swing of her hips. As she strode along, he noticed there was something off in her gait. She was wearing calf-high black boots and seemed slightly off-balance in them. Like maybe they were too large for her feet, or she just wasn't used to them. Just as she was disappearing around the corner, she looked back and waved goodbye to him with a thin smile and a twinkle in her dark eyes. And then Sahira was gone.

Charley set the plate on a small table in his room and pulled up a chair. The heady, rich smell of the stew hit him hard, and he dug in. Forkful after perfectly spiced forkful of meat, broth, vegetables and rice. He cracked open the last of his beers, now warmed to room temperature, and chugged it along with the stew. The meat was curious. He couldn't quite tell what it was, but it had a vague pork-like flavor and texture to it, so he decided it was probably pork. Maybe beef. But whatever it was, it filled him up.

Next to the table, a credenza held a large tube TV that had seen better days. He considered turning it on, vegging out for a while, but his eyes were drooping, and fatigue had returned. Checking his watch, he saw it was now nearly 2:30 a.m. Charley scraped the last of the stew and rice up from the plate and shoved it into his mouth, swallowing it down with the last mouthful of beer.

He dragged himself across the room, feet shuffling in the pile carpet. He opened the door into the chilly night air and left the plate outside the room. The moon glared down at him from the sky like the pallid dead eye of a fish left out in the sun. He closed the door and locked it, throwing the chain for good measure.

After turning off the light, he stripped off his jeans and shirt, pulled back the bedspread and collapsed onto the dingy bed. It smelled stale, somewhat musty, but he was too tired to care. Charley dragged the covers over himself and was asleep in moments.

He dreamed. Dark dreams of an endless wasteland under a burning red sky. Visions of crumbling tombstones, and shadowy, worm-like things slithering in the muck at the bottom of empty graves. And something lurking, slinking amongst the stones. A presence felt but unseen, creeping from tombstone to tombstone, closer to him with every passing moment.

By the time Charley woke later that day, the sun was already high in the sky. Golden light stretched like long fingers through the crack at the bottom and around the edges of the curtains he'd pulled tight the night before. His mouth was dry, his head ached, and his bladder was full.

Charley sat slowly up in bed, swung his feet to the floor and rubbed his head. As he lowered his hands, he once again noticed the dark crust under his nails. He picked at it a bit, then dug a tarnished multi-tool out from his duffel bag. Using the flat screwdriver attachment, he scraped the dry blood out from under the edges of his nails, watching it flake away and fall onto the carpet between his feet.

His stomach growled. Looking at the clock, he saw it was past two o'clock in the afternoon. He was definitely taking a detour on his way home.

Half an hour later, he'd taken a hot shower, scrubbing away the last of the crud under his fingernails, and went out in search of food.

When Charley opened the door and stepped out into the daylight, the sun momentarily blinded him. He lowered his head, shading his eyes while he fished around in his jacket pocket for a pair of dark Wayfarer-stye sunglasses. The dark lenses cut the glare almost instantly, and he stepped off the curb of the walkway which ran around the motel. He had parked his truck across from his room, and he walked over to check the coolers in the bed.

As he approached his truck, he saw that someone had knocked the coolers around during the night. He looked into the bed and saw that they were all open. Lids torn from hinges, the casings scratched all to hell. "Shit," he muttered.

Charley leaned over the side of the cargo bed and grabbed one cooler, dragging it closer to him. Looking inside, he saw smears of thin grey that looked like dried mucus. *Like snail trails*, he thought. Or like some slobbering dogs had been licking the inside. Charley dropped the cooler back to the truck bed and wiped his hands on his jeans. He looked around at the desolation surrounding the motel, the low, rocky fields across the road from him. “Coyotes,” he grumbled. “Bet it was freakin’ coyotes.”

The coolers were ruined, and he began thinking about how to dispose of them. He could probably dump them one at a time at highway rest stops while he finished the drive home tomorrow. Maybe see if he could ditch one today somewhere.

Charley’s stomach growled again, loud and persistent. He remembered Sahira mentioning there was a diner up the road and decided he’d go find it. A greasy burger and a cold beer sounded great all of a sudden.

He climbed into the truck and soon was back on the road; the vehicle shaking as he drove east on the rough, cracked asphalt. The Motel was still in his rearview mirror when he saw the road widen in front of the gates to a cemetery coming up on the right. A low, weathered masonry wall surrounded the small necropolis, but the gate was tall and ornate. Black wrought iron stretched up ten feet and arced over, stone monuments on either side. And tombstones scattered like broken teeth beyond it. As he passed by, he saw one monument which bracketed the gate, adorned with a weathered metal plaque embossed with “Pioneer Cemetery.”

He slowed the truck, looked in the rearview mirror to make sure nobody was behind him, then backed up until he was in front of the gate. There was no parking lot, but a wide patch of gravel and dirt in front of the gates looked like it would hold half a dozen cars. Probably for school field trips and people interested in early California history, he figured.

Charley got out of the truck and walked over to the gate. There was no lock on it, just a small latch to hold the thing closed. Probably more to keep out animals than horny teenagers. He grabbed one of the coolers out of the back of the truck, and proceeded to carry it around the side of the cemetery’s wall. The cemetery was desolate, decrepit. When he got around to the back, the area furthest from the road, he spotted some broken bottles of Coors beer and Fireball whiskey, and a dozen or more crushed cans of Budweiser. He dumped the cooler there amongst the detritus, kicking some dirt over it to complete the camouflage. Now anyone who saw it would think teenage partiers had left it behind. It was out of sight from the road, anyway.

He started the walk back toward the truck and glanced into the graveyard as he trudged along the rough dirt path. The grave markers here in the rear section of the cemetery were weather worn, ancient. *Probably over a hundred years old*, he thought. He checked a date on one and could barely make out that the person in the grave, one Jacob Riley, had died in either *188– or 186–*. The third digit was rough and worn, and the last was illegible. The ground before it was sunken in, bowed half a foot or more below the level of the dirt surrounding it. He looked at the next grave, and the one past that. All of them bowed in, like the coffins below had collapsed into the earth.

And beyond that, a black hole in the ground, open like a snarling mouth, the tombstone above it similarly ancient, weathered with age and neglect. But the grave before it hollowed out and empty.

And as the wind changed direction, he caught a whiff of foul air. A rotten, musty smell, like something left too long at the back of a fridge. The smell of rot, of death. It wasn't the first time he'd smelled that, of course. It reminded him of doing a disposal run on a hot day, the coolers laden with human remains baking in the sun in his truck bed on the way to dump them out.

And then he saw a flash of movement. Something pale, gray, lean and quick. It darted from behind one tombstone to another, low to the ground. He couldn't quite make out the shape in the distance. And with the obscuring stones between him and the thing, he couldn't quite discern a shape. He thought it might be a coyote or other wild dog. Then a high, quick bark sounded from the direction of the creature. Another quickly followed, then a series of yips and barks from the opposite side of the cemetery. When a third bark sounded from even closer, Charley picked up his pace toward the truck again.

As another breeze of fouled air wafted past, the hairs on the back of his neck twitched and gooseflesh ran up his back. He cast his eyes around the cemetery and began walking faster. Another cacophony of yips and barks made him look back over his shoulder. When he saw a brief flash of movement near the empty grave, he doubled his pace. Charley was almost running when he got back to his truck.

By the time Charley got to the Wagon Wheel diner and had his late lunch (or early dinner), he'd calmed significantly. The food was bland, and he ate it unceremoniously. Steak and eggs off the all-day breakfast menu, a side of fries, and a cold beer. But it had all tasted flat, flavorless, almost musty. Unsatisfying, at the very least. He'd drowned the food in ketchup, but even that didn't add any flavor.

He mopped at the smear of ketchup on his plate with an overly salted French fry, then popped the fry in his mouth. It tasted like nothing in particular. He swallowed the last of the beer, which just tasted like slightly yeasty water, then signaled the woman behind the diner counter for another. Even if it tasted flat, he could feel it working on him. His head was becoming deliciously fuzzy.

The woman—*Margery*, he saw on her name tag—returned with another glass. "Everything okay?" she asked, as he took the glass and downed half of it in a long gulp.

Charley shrugged. “Everything tastes off,” he said.

She raised one eyebrow and looked at his plate. “Well, you ate all of it, so don’t think about asking for a refund.”

He leaned back on his stool and glared at her. “No, it’s not spoiled or anything. I just can’t seem to taste it hardly at all.”

She tore his order check off of a little green receipt pad and handed it to him. “You must be coming down with something,” she said. “Maybe go home and get some sleep.”

He swallowed the rest of the beer. “Yeah,” he replied. “That must be it.”

Margery turned away, grabbing the glass pot off the coffeemaker, and went about refilling another customer’s cup, giving Charley a wary glance as she did.

Charley looked at the check, fished a twenty-dollar bill out of his wallet and left it on top of the check for the meal.

What he really wanted was more of the stew Sahira had given him the night before. Suddenly his mouth was filled with a phantom of the flavor of the spices, broth and meat. His stomach growled and he was hungry again. He stepped from his stool to leave and stopped when his feet hit the ground and he’d turned toward the exit.

Wide glass windows looked out onto the parking lot and road outside the diner. When he’d come in, the sun was still making its afternoon descent. But now the sky was black, speckled with stars, and the moon hung swollen and full overhead.

Charley walked outside, checked his watch and realized it was almost eight o’clock. He’d been in the diner for hours. No wonder the server had been giving him the stink-eye. As he walked from the diner, he saw a large dumpster at the side of the building. For a moment, he thought about dumping one of the empty coolers in it but decided against that. Margery had already seemed suspicious enough. Better not to push his luck.

The light of the moon washed the parking lot in a silver glow as Charley got back into his truck and started back to the motel. His mini-vacation was turning into more hassle than it was worth. All he wanted to do was crash out for the night and get on his way first thing in the morning.

When he got back to the motel, he thought about packing up his stuff and bailing right then. It was only another hour to his apartment, and he was warming to the idea of heading east, of starting his life anew. But he decided to stick it out for one more night. He was still exhausted, still road-worn. One more night to rest up was what he needed.

Charley turned on the bedside lamp, flopped on the bed, and reached for the remote control on the bedside table. He thumbed the power button on the remote and after a moment the channel menu came on. Scrolling through the channels didn't present him with anything even slightly interesting. He thought about the two coolers still in the back of his truck and wondered again about how he'd go about disposing of them. He thought about the future, and what it might look like. Settle down somewhere in the middle of nowhere. Maybe meet a nice girl, start a family. The whole white-picket-fence deal.

Then the TV and lamp both went dead. He checked the clock radio on the bedside stand and it was out too. Power was out through his room. Some dim light still glowed around the edges of the curtains. *Probably the lights in the parking lot and the full moon*, he thought.

As his mind wandered, a knock at the door startled him out of his musing. He sat up in bed and looked toward the door. When he was fully upright, he heard a soft shuffling. Like the bedsheets ruffling against the pile of the carpet. Or something moving under the bed.

He vaulted off the bed, landing almost in front of the door, and then instinctively flipped the switch on for the overhead light, but of course no light came. The knock came again at the door. Reaching out, he felt for the doorknob, fumbling until he found and gripped it. He kept his eyes on the bed until the last moment as he turned the knob and opened the door.

Sahira stood outside, backlit by the parking lot lights as he opened the door. "Power's out," she said.

"Yeah, I noticed," Charley replied. "Any idea what happened?"

She shook her head, glossy black hair shimmering with reflected light. "No, not at all." He barely noticed her peek over his shoulder, like she was examining the room for something.

Charley turned to see what she was looking at, but stopped when she spoke again.

"It's only affecting part of the motel too," she said. "There's still power in the office and front of the building."

"Well," he said. "I was turning in anyway. Probably going to hit the road early tomorrow."

"Nonsense," she said, stepping forward. "You're the only guest here tonight, and I feel bad you being all alone in the dark." She placed her hand on his chest, ran her fingers up the side of his neck. She leaned in and breathed in deep, like she was smelling him. Then she exhaled, breath tickling the fine hairs on his neck.

A moment later, the stench hit his nostrils. A fetid stink filled his sinuses, oozed down his throat into his lungs. As she pulled back, he saw tendrils of poisonous green fog trickling from her mouth. Her eyes glowed silver like the moon. He felt his face go cold, numb. Then his muscles went slack.

"Besides," she said. "My family would just love to have you for dinner." His knees buckled, and she pushed him with both hands. He took a fumbling step back but stumbled over something right behind his calves. The world went cockeyed as he stumbled backward, falling, bouncing off the mattress and then slamming his forehead on the bedside table. Stars swam before his eyes as he fell to the floor, his face pressed into the carpet. He could just barely feel icy hands grip his wrists and pull them behind him, lashing them together.

And then the smell. The same ripe, dead smell from the cemetery earlier. Close, overpowering. Something cracked into the back of his skull, and everything went dark.

Charley's mind was adrift in abstract, cloudy green seas of indistinct patterns and abstract shapes. Slowly he swam to the surface of consciousness.

As he became aware, he realized that he was lying down on something flat and hard. He blinked, eyes gritty and dry as he opened them and tried to focus. Above him a fuzzy redness, which slowly solidified into a bloom of silks suspended from the ceiling. He was in a small room, no bigger than the hotel room he'd spent the previous night in. Turning his head from side to side, he saw the walls were draped with the same scarlet silks, giving the impression of a luxurious tent. The area was illuminated by small flames, erupting from ornate brass lamps arrayed in a circle around him. Each lamp hung from brass chains, which reached up to disappear in the silks.

His body felt slightly numb, as if he'd been shot up all over with lidocaine, and it was just wearing off. Charley tried to sit up, only then realizing his wrists and ankles had been tied down with leather thongs. He was lashed to a slab of wood, raised about four feet above the ground.

Then came a slithering whisper as the silk barrier parted beyond his feet. A dark slit opened in the shimmering redness, and Sahira slunk through. "You're awake," she said, walking toward him. She tugged on the thongs holding down his feet and they did not give.

"Hey, lady, I don't know what kind of pervy game you think you're playing here, but I'm not down for it," Charley said. "Why don't you just let me go and I'll be on my way."

She approached, leaning over his face. He caught a whiff of her as she did. Under the sweet musky smell of her perfume, a hint of decay, a stink of putrefaction. Like a piece of rotting meat that had been over-spiced to hide the corruption. "Oh, no," she said. "You're not going anywhere just yet. You're the guest of honor tonight."

Charlie struggled against the thongs. "You have no idea who you're messing with, woman!" he shouted. "You've got no idea the kinds of folks I'm friends with."

"Well," she said, leaning back and stepping away from him. "Isn't that a coincidence?"

From all around him, the silk walls parted and a nightmarish menagerie stepped through. Five semi-human shapes surrounded him, and the miasma of rot flowed through the chamber. The creatures were not as tall as Sahira. One was much shorter, almost child-sized. But as Charley watched, it grew, bones and sinews creaking and groaning as it expanded until it matched the height of the others.

"What the hell are they?" Charley said, his voice barely above a whisper.

"My family," Sahira said. "In older times, people called us ghûls. Now we're mostly forgotten. Quaint memories of folktales, used to scare naughty children. But as you can see, we're altogether real. And they've been dying to meet you."

The beings were dressed simply in cotton pants and open-chested linen shirts. Their skin was rough, dry and almost scaly in patches, warty and knobby in others. One's face was almost human, except for the glittering dark eyes like those of a fly or some other loathsome insect. Two of them bore strange, horn-like growths on their foreheads, another had a ridge of spines which trailed from the center of its forehead over its skull. The only common feature to them all was a strange stooped posture, as if they were leaning forward ready to pounce, balanced on the balls of their feet. But no, not feet. From his prone position, Charley could just see that where toes should be, they stood on solid, thick hooves.

One of the hybrid creatures turned and spoke to Sahira in a language Charley couldn't understand. When it finished speaking, it turned its head to glare at Charley, then smiled a terrible grin, exposing a mouth full of glistening, knife-sharp teeth. Sahira responded in kind, causing all the creatures to throw their heads back in barking laughter.

Sahira turned back to Charley, drawing a long, curved silver knife from behind her back as she did. She slashed at the thongs holding down his legs, then the ones at his hands. Then she spoke: "Run."

Charley bolted upright, leapt from the slab and landed on his bare feet next to it. One creature reached out a gnarled, clawed hand and drew aside the silk drapes. Beyond, Charley saw blackness and diamond speckles of stars in the night sky. He took a step toward the opening and the creature smiled, leaning forward almost in a bow.

One other behind him barked out something that caused the rest to cackle in high-pitched, yowling laughter. The thing holding the silks open gestured with its other hand as if to say to Charley, "Please, after you."

Charley took three steps toward the opening, then he turned to face the creatures as he backed out of the chamber. He saw Sahira and the creatures leaning forward, expectantly. They all glared at him, their eyes filled with hungry intent. A thin thread of drool dripped from one's wolfish maw.

Charley took one step backward and was outside in the night air. He saw the things inside hunch down like runners starting a race. As he watched they changed, their forms fluid, hands becoming paw-like, spines extending, jaws jutted forward. All but Sahira, who stayed immutable, walking behind the beast-like things as they slunk forward toward the exit Charley had just walked through.

He turned and bolted into the night, across the sandy, rocky ground. The moon overhead washed the sparse terrain with a silver glow. His legs pumped, feet tearing up the ground as he ran.

And then a howl from behind him. Singular at first, then followed by companion voices. He looked over his shoulder to see the five creatures a hundred yards behind and rushing toward him. Beyond them, the red silk tent glowed like a dying coal in a campfire. He kept running, looking side to side, trying to find the road, a house or structure, anywhere he could hide out. But there was nothing. He was in wide open space with the awful creatures bearing down on him.

He was running, directionless, when he stumbled over a low branch and plowed face-first into the dirt. Pain exploded in his tongue as he bit it. He pushed himself up and felt blood running from his nose and tasted it in his mouth. He rose to his knees and was suddenly surrounded by the creatures.

One rushed him, tackling him and biting his shoulder. Blood gushed down Charley's back as the thing leapt away. Then another slashed at him with its cruelly barbed claws, splitting the denim over Charley's thigh, and drawing a deep gash through skin and muscle. Blood flowed. The creatures stepped aside, widening their circle around him.

Seeing an opening, Charley staggered forward as the creatures yipped and barked. He limped away, and when he looked behind, saw them inching along after him on all fours, their heads low to the ground, snarling with animal malevolence.

Charley tried to move faster, but his head was swimming, he was feeling faint. Blood soaked his jeans below the gash in his leg and was gushing from his shoulder. Something pounced on his back, knocking him to the dusty ground. He smelled the foul breath of one of the ghûls at his neck, felt its weight on his back. Then searing pain as it nipped at his scalp, tearing away a strip of skin. Then the weight was gone, and Charley lay face down in the dirt.

He slowly rolled onto his back. He saw the creatures closing in from all sides. Then Sahira strode through the pack toward him.

"They like you, you know," she said. "They think maybe you could be one of us."

"Us?" Charley said, and blood flowed from his mouth. "You're one of them, too?"

"Not exactly," Sahira said. "But close enough. And I could make you like them. I've seen into your heart. I know what you are, and what you could be."

Charley got up onto one elbow. "To hell with you," he said.

"Been there," Sahira replied. "It didn't stick."

He tried to rise, but his leg gave out, and he fell back to the dust. Sahira stepped forward and placed her boot on his chest, pressing him into the ground.

"Why'd you let me go if they were just going to chase me down?" Charlie asked.

"Ghûls are curious creatures," she said. "They like to play with their food. And it's been ages since they had fresh meat."

In a frenzy of claws and teeth they descended on Charley, rending, biting and clawing. Tearing him limb from limb, splitting joints with their teeth, stripping skin and organs from bone. As his mind faded, he imagined wide open spaces, and a brief image of himself sitting on a rocking chair on the porch of a lonely country house. Then final, all-consuming darkness overcame him.

Soon there was nothing left but his splintered skeleton under the night sky, and the ghûls fought over the last scraps. They cracked the bones and sucked the marrow until the shards were dry and clean.

As the sun rose over the hills in the east, the pack of ghûls dug a shallow hole in the dusty ground and tossed the bones within. No carrion creatures would disturb the mound, for they knew the scent of evil. By the time the sun was high in the sky, the low patch had baked dry, and Charley Watson was nothing more than dust.

Known as a "hopping vampire"
Kills by absorbing life force
Infects victims via a "virus"
How to destroy: • Use a mirror – terrified of their own reflections
• Use wood from a peach tree as a weapon.
• Drop a bag of coins – the vampire will be compelled to count every coin.

MR. HOP IN WONGTOWN

Lisa Morton

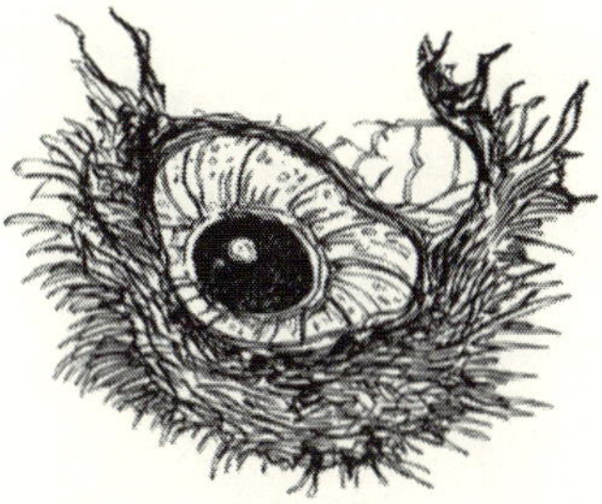

The sun had just set behind the Hong Kong hills and WongTown when Jimmy Ryan first saw the hopping vampire.

It was strange synchronicity, because the young American had been wandering the decaying backlot of the Wong Brothers' venerable studio and thinking: *WongTown is haunted.*

Of course it was haunted for him. Even though this was Jimmy's first trip to Hong Kong and to the studio fondly referred to as "WongTown," he knew it intimately, its streets and structures, its inns and shops and temples and palaces. He'd first fallen in love with martial arts films when he was fourteen and had stumbled on a dubbed pan-and-scan version of Chang Cheh's classic *Deadly Fingers of Death*. Now he was here, as a screenwriter whose script *Lotus Sword, Buddha Staff* would soon go into production in WongTown. He stood in the middle of a shadowed street, allowing himself to drink it all in, reveling in the sights, sounds, smells, the feel of it all.

He was just noticing a doorway that he was pretty sure Ti Lung had been thrown out of in *The One-Armed Boxer* when he saw movement out of the corner of his eye. He'd been told that Wong-Town was deserted, since the company that had acquired both his script and the legendary studio hadn't secured all their financing yet. In fact, other than two security guards at the front gate, he hadn't seen so much as a maintenance man in the thirty minutes since he'd arrived, having come straight from the Chek Lap Kok airport on Lantau Island. He turned, seeking the source of the movement, but the evening dusk was starting to settle over the dilapidated buildings, and Jimmy didn't see whatever had drawn his attention.

Jimmy wondered if this area was safe after dark; had some of the crumbling structures been infested by animals, or become homes to the homeless? He was supposed to meet Tony Chan, the famed fight choreographer who would be directing *Lotus Sword, Buddha Staff* and whose assistant Cheng Siu-ma had picked him up at the airport, at the front offices in fifteen minutes; maybe that glimpse of movement had been Tony, arrived early.

"Tony?" Jimmy called out, but received no answer.

Shrugging, he decided to step into one of the buildings. Most of the furnishings had long since been removed, but Jimmy still recognized the round windows and the huge ceramic wine urns stacked against one wall—this set had once hosted an astonishing fistfight between Lo Lieh and Alexander Fu Sheng in *The Five Deadly Venoms Vs. Shaolin.*

It was too dark to make out much detail. Still, Jimmy took his time, just breathing in the atmosphere, imagining what it had been like fifty years earlier; he could almost see the ghosts of cameramen and stuntmen and actors moving across the dust-covered floorboards. He used a flashlight app on his phone to examine a wall, which was covered in slash marks apparently made by real swords. He laughed in sheer joy.

A shadow crossed the wall.

Jimmy turned, some instinct telling him to remain silent. Moving cautiously, he approached one of the round windows, looked outside—and stared in disbelief.

There was a man in the street, hopping.

Hopping just like the Chinese vampires—the *geung-si*—in the *Mr. Hop* series, with his arms held out stiffly before him, knees barely bending.

This man, though, wasn't dressed in any antiquated Ching Dynasty burial robes and black hat like the cinematic Asian monsters, but what looked in the low light to be a modern business suit. Even in the gloom Jimmy could see that his skin was pale, his features drawn, the suit dirty and tattered.

Each hop forward carried him at least fifteen feet.

Jimmy's first thought was that he'd walked in on a production, possibly even a new *Mr. Hop* film. Why hadn't anyone told him? Had he already spoiled a shot? And why was the actor dressed in modern day clothing, yet surrounded by 18th century buildings?

Jimmy poked his head out farther, looking for the wire rig that was obviously allowing the actor to make such prodigious hops.

He didn't see anything. Then it occurred to him …

Where were the lights? Was the crew hiding? Why?

Jimmy was still standing at the window, staring, when the actor (*or whatever*, thought Jimmy with growing unease) suddenly stopped, executed a ninety-degree turn in small leaps, and stood facing Jimmy, perhaps fifty feet away.

It began hopping towards him.

Jimmy stumbled back in panic. How could anyone have seen him in the almost-total darkness of the building interior? He'd already pocketed his phone, and he'd been utterly silent.

And why was the strange figure coming *right at him*?

A joke. This had to be a joke, probably orchestrated by Tony Chan—in fact, hadn't one of Tony's first films as a director been *Mr. Hop 4*?

"Ha-ha, very funny," he called out, then added a Cantonese phrase he'd learned from all the movies, "*ho siu.*"

Then the smell hit him.

He nearly gagged. It was a terrible rotting meat odor, acrid and sweet at the same time. When Jimmy was a kid, he'd once hidden in a half-full trash bin behind a butcher shop to escape a bully, and it had smelled something like this.

That smell was coming from the thing that was now ten feet away.

Jimmy froze again, all thoughts of jokes overwhelmed by an instinctive fear of the scent of death. The thing hopped to the window and peered in at Jimmy.

Its eyes glowed slightly.

Jimmy was glad the window was too small for it to hop through.

It turned and he knew it was heading for the entrance.

Jimmy didn't stop to consider the impossibility of what he was seeing; instead, his mind raced back through the *Mr. Hop* films, trying to recall how the bumbling heroes of those movies had escaped the reanimated, hopping cadavers.

They'd held up eight-sided mirrors.

He obviously didn't have one of those.

A string blessed by a Taoist ritual.

None of those handy, either.

Then he remembered: in the movies, the *geung-si* tracked the heroes by following their breathing; to escape, the protagonists could simply hold their breath. This, of course, had led to much hilarity as the camera lingered on actors with puffed-out cheeks frantically pinching their noses shut.

Okay, fine, Jimmy thought, *I'll play along.*

As the vampire appeared in the doorway, Jimmy inhaled deeply and sealed his lips.

The *geung-si* froze.

Jimmy stifled an insane urge to howl laughter. *This is ridiculous. They've taken some stunt guy, rubbed him in dead meat, and sent him out here just to pull a fastie on the gullible American ... I'm getting royally punked while they're laughing somewhere.*

But he didn't release his breath.

Suddenly a young male voice sounded outside, perhaps fifty yards distant. "Jimmy … Jimmy Ryan, are you out here? Tony's looking for you … Jimmy?"

Jimmy recognized the voice as belonging to Cheng Siu-ma, Tony's assistant/interpreter. Jimmy didn't respond.

But the vampire did. It turned in ridiculous little jumps then started hopping in the direction of the voice.

Still holding his breath, Jimmy ran up to the doorway and looked out.

The *geung-si* had hopped to the middle of the street just as Siu-ma appeared. "Jimmy, are you … uh …"

Siu-ma saw the creature and broke off, first gaping in disbelief, then laughing. "*Wah! Ho ho!*"

The *geung-si* jumped again and sank its long nails into Siu-ma's shoulders.

The young man's laughter abruptly shattered, leaving him to stare in mute horror as the vampire's mouth fell open, its dead eyes fixed on Siu-ma's. Siu-ma struggled briefly, then there was a sound like rushing wind as a reddish mist began to flow from Siu-ma to the *geung-si*.

Jimmy knew the horrible thing was feeding on the helpless young man, stealing his *chi*, his life essence.

Again, he thought back to the *Mr. Hop* films, trying desperately to recall how the *geung-si* had been stopped. There'd been something involving rice, and …

Jimmy suddenly remembered: *The only ones who could stop the vampires were Taoist sorcerers.*

Unfortunately, there didn't seem to be any of those around right now, either.

While Jimmy was trying to decide what to do, the *geung-si* abruptly released Siu-ma. The victim slumped to the ground, and the vampire hopped over the body, away from Jimmy.

Apparently, it was full.

Jimmy waited until it had completely disappeared, then he ran to Siu-ma and knelt over him. Jimmy reached down and his fingers brushed against Siu-ma's face, which was slick with blood, but Siu-ma was still alive.

Jimmy nearly gagged and stumbled back. He reached for his phone before realizing he had no idea who to call—did Hong Kong have 911?

Instead, he got to his feet and ran.

Two hours later, Siu-ma had been taken to the hospital, and Jimmy had finished giving the police his report. He told them only that he hadn't seen much of the man who had attacked Siu-ma: it'd been too dark.

After the police left, Tony Chan and the producer who'd bought Jimmy's script, Martin Wong, held their own interrogation in Martin's office (which had once belonged to Wong "Daai-goh," one of the original two Wong Brothers). It was Jimmy's first time meeting either of them in person, after months of phone calls and

Zoom conferences; Chan still possessed the wiry frame of a semi-retired stuntman, and Wong was middle-aged but still hip in shades and leather jacket. Jimmy desperately wished their first meeting hadn't involved him confessing that he'd just witnessed a hopping vampire.

"What do you mean?" Martin asked.

"Well … he hopped. And he looked—and smelled—dead."

They both stared at Jimmy in disbelief.

"*Geung-si*," muttered Tony.

"*Geung-si*," Jimmy agreed.

"*Fai wa*," Tony said, shaking his head. His tone and gesture told Jimmy that wasn't such a nice phrase.

"Jimmy," Martin (whose English was far better than Tony's) said, "I know you're a big fan of all the old movies, but … don't fuck with us."

"I'm not—"

Just then Martin's phone rang (Jimmy recognized the tune as the theme song from *Once Upon a Time in China*), and the producer snapped it up to his face. "Yeah …"

His eyes narrowed slightly as he listened. "Bring him here."

He snapped the phone closed again. "That was security. They said some guy just showed up at the front gate claiming to know about the attack. Let's see what we've got."

The trio was silent while they waited for the informant to arrive, and Jimmy's thoughts kept circling back to what he'd seen.

He believed. He'd seen a real *geung-si*.

The *Mr. Hop* films had been ludicrous, with broad comedic scenes that were more often eye-rolling than funny, but they'd been based on *something*, hadn't they? Even if what he'd seen had been a stuntman on a wire-rig, a man really was in the hospital.

If the *geung-si* were real … what else was? Jimmy had been raised a good Baptist boy from Texas; even though he hadn't been in a church in at least five years, he still believed. But, if the eastern vampires were real, then what about the eastern gods? What about kung fu, and people who could use *chi* to fly?

His thoughts were interrupted by a knock on the office door, followed by the entrance of a uniformed security guard … leading a man dressed in the yellow robes and huge eight-sided medallion of a Taoist monk.

Martin, Tony and Jimmy all stared speechlessly as the monk bowed deeply, holding up one hand in a two-fingered greeting or blessing.

Martin and the monk conversed briefly in Cantonese before they both looked at Jimmy, and Martin asked, "Do you speak English?"

The monk nodded. "Yes. I am Lam Man-kong."

Jimmy was struck by both the monk's resemblance to the actor who'd played the Taoist sorcerer in the *Mr. Hop* movies, and the odd fact that the actor and monk shared the same surname. The monk had a serious face, with heavy graying brows that formed a single line over his eyes, and a strong, jutting chin.

Martin motioned to the security guard, who left, then he turned to the Taoist. "Are you a priest, or a …?"

"I am humble monk, sir, from Taoist temple in Shenzhen. For some time now I follow *geung-si*."

Martin shot Jimmy a look before turning back to Lam. "*Geung-si*?"

Lam nodded. "I believe in English is 'vampire'."

"And you're following it?"

Again, a single sharp nod. "Yes. *Geung-si* is born because improper burial. I follow it so it can go back to home village and have proper burial. Then it will really die."

Tony suddenly rose halfway from his chair, snarling something at the monk. The monk bowed his head and made the two-fingered gesture again, while he murmured something that sounded vaguely familiar to Jimmy; he thought it was some kind of prayer.

Martin motioned Tony back and stepped forward himself. "You know a man was badly hurt here tonight?"

The monk gestured at Tony. "He tell me. I am very sorry. I can help."

"How?"

"*Geung-si* return tomorrow, looking for victim again. I catch *geung-si*, and return to village."

Martin asked, "And how will you do that?"

The monk removed a long scrap of yellow paper from his robes. "I write sutra on paper, then place paper on *geung-si* head. Then it obey me."

Martin shook his head, and then fixed the monk with a hard stare. "Okay, joke's over. What studio are you from?"

The monk looked perplexed. "I do not understand question—"

Martin shouted, "Who put you up to this?!"

"Oh. *Ming baak, ming baak* … You need proof."

Martin laughed. "Yeah, that'd help."

The monk considered briefly, then abruptly put a finger to his teeth and nipped the skin. He made a sign in the air with his crimsoned fingertip—and then leapt forward and jammed the bloody digit against Jimmy's forehead.

Martin and Tony were both out of their chairs and grabbing at Lam as Jimmy staggered back, swiping frantically at his brow.

"*Chi sin ah*!" said Martin, as the monk deftly evaded his grasp.

"He has mark now. *Geung-si* come for him tomorrow night, but I stop *geung-si*. You see and believe."

The monk turned and left.

Tony and Martin both turned to Jimmy, who was rubbing away the blood now staining his fingers. "I'm okay," he said, warding off the questions.

But he was lying; he wasn't okay.

In fact, he was terrified.

Jimmy struggled the next day to work with Tony on the script, but he couldn't concentrate.

In the warm light of day, it was hard to accept the existence of anything as impossible as a resurrected hopping corpse seeking to drain the living of their *chi*; but Jimmy knew dusk was coming, and even though he'd scrubbed his forehead until it was raw, he couldn't help but feel that he'd been somehow tainted.

The monk had said it: he'd been *marked.*

As late afternoon drew to a close, Tony suddenly clapped Jimmy on the shoulder, and rattled off a string of Cantonese. A new assistant—since Siu-ma was in the hospital—translated for Jimmy, and told him that Tony was suggesting they spend the night touring the busy district of Tsim Sha Tsui, away from the lot. Tony knew a great restaurant; afterwards, they could try some of the area's famed clubs, get drunk, sing karaoke, rent a cheap hotel room for the night.

Jimmy was relieved; surely he'd be safe in an active urban area, surrounded by people?

It turned out to be just Tony and Jimmy climbing into Tony's SUV and heading down the mountain, but Jimmy realized they didn't need the interpreter; they were already developing a strange communication method made up of one-part Cantonese, one-part English, and two-parts body language. Jimmy guessed he was in for a special evening.

He was right. Three hours later, after an amazing dinner of noodles and congee at Tony's favorite hole-in-the-wall *chan gwoon*, and a half-dozen bottles of Tsing Tao each at the first club (which Jimmy recognized as the setting from a recent crime drama, *Triad Killer*), they were staggering onto Tsim Sha Tsui's crowded night-time sidewalks, all thoughts of hopping vampires vanquished by the search for the next club. They clung to each other, laughing at the stares and muttered imprecations they drew from passersby as they banged elbows or shoulders.

They left Cameron Road, heading past herb shops with open barrels of dried scallops and triad street vendors hawking burner phones, and turned onto busy Nathan Road, with its overpriced electronics shops and tailors targeted at naïve tourists. They were heading towards the harbor when Jimmy caught a glimpse of weird movement on the sidewalk in front of them.

Hopping movement.

He instantly felt his stomach clench, and his pleasant drunkenness vanished. He stopped, trying desperately to see through the crowd. Tony stumbled forward a few feet before realizing Jimmy was no longer with him. He turned and looked at Jimmy curiously.

Jimmy didn't notice. He'd seen another hop. Just for a second. Just a quick image, burned into his retinas now, of a head that had popped up above the crowd, a head with a pale face and dead eyes.

"It's here," Jimmy said, trying to squelch panic.

"*Mat ye ah*?" asked Tony, his words slurred.

The crowd behind Tony parted. Jimmy heard cries of alarm, shouts, laughter.

The *geung-si* hopped, sightlessly, through the throngs on the sidewalk, heading for Jimmy.

Jimmy tried to turn and run, but discovered that the rest of his body hadn't sobered up with his head. His feet tangled around each other and he went down as the *geung-si* approached.

Tony spun, seeing it for the first time. Instead of fear or astonishment, he grinned, crouched, thrust one fist forward.

Oh my God, he's not going to try to fight that thing—

Then Jimmy realized that Tony still thought this was some stunt man, or practical joker; Tony was a former real-life martial arts champion, and probably thought that, even drunk, he could teach this idiot a lesson.

What happened next was a blur that Jimmy saw through a haze of fear and alcohol: the *geung-si,* still dressed in that fraying suit, hopped forward, and Tony threw a punch into its midsection. It reached out with one of those clawed, extended arms and picked Tony up by the shoulder, dangling him effortlessly. Around them, a crowd had formed, cheering and applauding; Jimmy heard the phrase "*Tiu Sin Saang*", and some part of him remembered that was the Chinese version of *Mr. Hop*.

The crowd had whipped out phones and were happily recording the scene, thinking this was some kind of promotion for a *Mr. Hop* movie.

The *geung-si* tossed Tony aside, and Tony crashed into a building wall, having missed going through a plate glass window by a foot. Then the *geung-si* continued on towards Jimmy.

He made one half-hearted effort to climb to his feet, but somehow he couldn't find them; all he could do was crouch back and stare, wide-eyed and shaking, as the dead thing in a fraying, stained suit that stank of death hopped to a halt before him and started to bend down, its jaw falling open, its eyes blazing … and then the yellow-robed monk was there, calmly plastering a strip of yellow paper with red calligraphy onto the *geung-si*'s head.

It froze.

The onlookers roared approval.

Lam turned and offered a hand to Jimmy, who took it, and somehow got to his feet. Tony was already rising, looking dazed and fearful. The monk crossed to him, whispered into his ear, and then Tony turned and walked off quickly.

"Where's he going?" Jimmy cried, ready to take off after his director.

"Bring back car, so we can take *geung-si* away."

Jimmy shrank back. "Oh, no, I'm not getting in a car with that thing—"

Then Jimmy leaned over and vomited into the gutter.

The crowd applauded again. The monk turned and bowed.

Tony and Lam didn't have any difficulty maneuvering the *geung-si* into the back area of the SUV. It was a large vehicle, and by folding down some of the seats they were able to lay it flat in the rear.

Jimmy rode in the front passenger seat, embarrassed, exhausted, hanging his head out the window, trying to avoid the death smell that now permeated the car's interior.

They returned to WongTown, and once they had the *geung-si* unloaded again, the monk was able to control its movements by ringing a bell—it would obediently hop forward or turn, depending on which direction he pointed as he rang. It didn't make any sense to Jimmy, but neither did a lot of things lately.

They found Martin Wong, to show him the *geung-si*. He felt its cold, brittle skin, held a finger up beneath its breathless nose, peered into its filmy eyes, and finally stepped back, shaking his head.

Then he turned to the monk, and they chatted in Cantonese. Jimmy listened, picking up a few words here and there but not really following the conversation. When Martin started to walk out of the room, Jimmy called out in alarm, "Where are you going?"

Martin paused in the doorway to explain: "The monk can take this thing away, but he needs money for burial expenses. He wants ten thousand Hong Kong dollars, in cash. I'll be right back." Martin walked out.

Jimmy turned to look at the monk, who bowed. "All praise to Buddha."

Jimmy nodded his head slowly, respectfully, hoping he'd done the right thing. The monk smiled.

Martin returned a few moments later with an envelope of cash for Lam. The monk actually counted it before he bowed.

A security man appeared, and Martin said, "Take this man and his—uh, companion—wherever they need to go." The guard nodded and turned to Lam, who rang the bell to direct the *geung-si* as they left, the monk bowing a final time.

The producer, director and screenwriter all collapsed into chairs, silent.

Finally Martin got up and found a bottle of Jack Daniels. He poured three shots and passed them around, then settled back behind his desk, contemplating.

"Shit," he murmured, "I wonder if I should've offered him a deal◦…"

A week later, they heard about an unusual incident that happened to a work crew building a resort on an outlying island:

One of their men was attacked by a thing that hopped. A monk showed up, said he could control the monster, but would need money for its burial.

That was when Martin realized he'd been had.

Jimmy expected him to be angry, but instead the producer just smiled. "I fell for it because he was a monk, but he's just a con man with a good scam. Shit."

"Well," Jimmy said, "it may have been a scam, but the *geung-si* was real."

"Yeah. That's what made the scam so good."

Later that day, Martin offered Jimmy his next job: They needed a screenwriter on *Mr. Hop Returns*. The little scene in Tsim Sha Tsui had garnered so much media attention that it seemed a shame to waste it.

Jimmy was thrilled. After everything he'd been through, he still loved WongTown and its legendary films; Hong Kong felt like home, and he thought he could be happy spending the rest of his life there making his own cinematic history. He was already starting to pick up some of the local Cantonese (after only a week he could curse fluently), and he loved the restaurants and clubs and shops and harbor and people.

He did tell Martin he'd need a short vacation before the next project, though. He needed to return home, see his family in Texas.

He thought he should be face to face with them when he broke the news that he was converting to Taoism.

THE HORSEMAN RIDES

Stephanie M. Wytovich

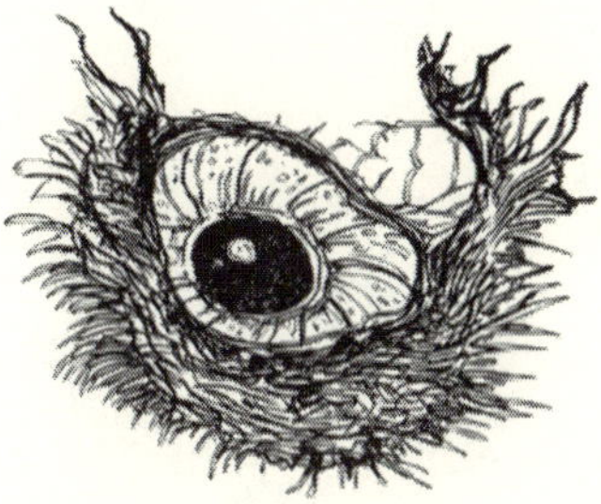

Out of the fog, he arrives,
a spider, a snake. There is no
stopping his blade, the pumpkins
carved, the apples bobbing,
their blood-red skin aflame by
candlelight.

Don't breathe, lock your doors,
the sound of bones, those arthritic
creaks, they'll give you away like
gun shots, like fire.

The forest prays for you, wishes
you hidden: a lost key, a forgotten book.

For he moves like smoke, a demon

in the night, his horse a black stallion,
the devil's compass leading straight
to you, your head a beacon, a coveted
jewel.

Now stand still, disappear if you can,
his axe is hungry, eager to sever,
to slice through warm flesh, your throat
the consequence of curses, of an agreement
made too many moons ago.

The village weeps for you, whispers
their apologies: we're sorry, we're sorry

a payment is due.

PLANETA MUMIA

Maxwell I. Gold

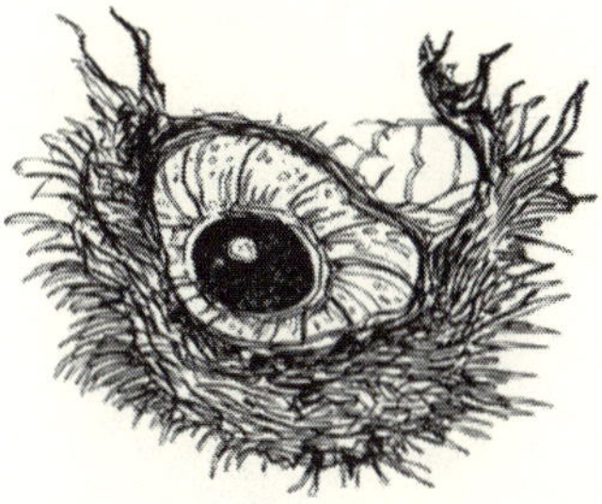

Confined to an infinity of rags and death, soaked in the tattered scars of some forgotten yesterday, I saw a planet buried and burned under the heaviness of its worshipful, lusty dread. No more were the streets clustered by the slaps and sweat from flesh-feet or bodies rich with blood and brazen youth, but the embalmed cadavers of tomorrow crowded cities of grave-dust and ash whose mouths belched plumes of moths, dirt, and slime.

Old houses, now tombs sparkling with the richness of a gilded past, carried onwards into the deep brown horizon underneath the moaning chorus of unhappy, ragged souls. Never were they forgiven for the atrocities committed, the lives taken, and so they were still doomed to wander all that remained, until the world decayed into atoms and stardust, and there was nothing left to say.

Nothing left of the planet confined to an infinity of rags and death, my tattered scars, soaked in some forgotten yesterday.

THE CORPSE EATER

Maxwell I. Gold

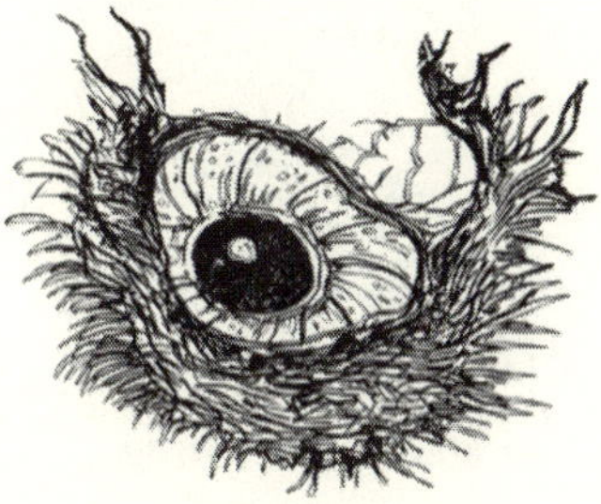

Muso's foot slipped, sending loose gravel over the edge of the ridge. He landed hard on one knee and yelped so loud it echoed in the lowland between the hills. Embarrassed, he immediately apologized to the Buddha for his inattentiveness.

The young monk glanced over the steep side and then behind him where something terrible skulked in the shadows. It had been stalking him ever since the sun dipped behind Mino Peak, about twenty minutes ago. Probably a wolf. Surely not one of the beasties the townspeople warned him about? He recalled yesterday, the dirty lot of them huddled around, repeating outrageous stories and warning him off the mountain. He'd smiled and quietly prayed that their irrational fears be taken away. If his studies had taught him anything at all, it was that none of this was real.

A twig snapped and reminded him with an icy crackle through his chest that it would be completely dark soon. Unreal or not, wolves got hungry. He needed to find the valley community, the rest point on the way to Enshu and the coast he had been wanting to see his whole life. He should have reached it by now. Was he lost?

Muso's hands trembled as he clicked juzu beads through his fingers and prayed. It wasn't a selfish prayer. He didn't ask for ease from the incredible torment he was in. No. He tried not to think about how thirsty, hungry, and exhausted he was and instead repeated the Heart Sutra and reminded himself of the impermanence of life. But also, he didn't want to die.

Muso pushed himself unsteadily to his feet with his walking stick and continued on. He'd been moving since sunrise. The straw chords of his waraji sandals bit into his ankles and the soft skin on the tops of his feet until they were sticky with blood. His leg muscles trembled. He swallowed nothing past his swollen tongue. Faith flagging, he was certain he was about to be devoured by a pack of wolves. Or at least one. Muso gently reminded the Buddha how a monk rended limb from limb was of no use spreading the holy Dharma.

He plodded on until a turn on the path stopped him in his tracks. Lit pink by the dying sun—as if set down by Shakyamuni himself—a one-room ramshackle hut. He hadn't come across one of these in years, a retreat for fellow monks who seek solitude to further their spiritual journey. This one had thin gray threads of smoke spiraling from the thatched roof. Someone was home.

Muso limped over, knocked and called out a greeting. The door creaked open and revealed the sun-spotted bald head of an elderly monk, his eyes pinched closed.

"Fellow brother in the Sangha," Muso began with a bow. "I have traveled far and am in need of a place to lie my head for the night. If I would be no bother—"

"Go away!" It wasn't anger that flashed across the elder monk's face, but something more like fear.

"Please don't be afraid. I'm not a bandit or a beast," Muso said. "I really am—

"Down there." A boney hand shot out from behind the door and pointed to the valley behind Muso. How did he miss it? The soft welcoming glow of paper lanterns and people milling about.

"They are kind folk. They will give you a place to stay and something to eat and drink. Hurry. It's dangerous on these trails after dark."

Muso understood the blind sage's reluctance to allow a stranger into his hut. He thanked him and with a burst of renewed energy, hurried along the path to the cluster of humble houses below.

Muso was half delirious by the time he reached the crowd of mumbling villagers. He called out and they all turned, paper lanterns raised, painting their faces in monstrous red dancing shadows. Relief washed over him. He took another step forward, stumbled, as all light was extinguished and fell.

A woman's cry. The sound of waraji stamping on hard-packed earth. Hushed, concerned voices, and hands pulling at his robes and arms. The feeling of being dragged. He remembered greedily drinking bitter tea, spilling it, then apologizing again to the Exalted One for his lack of composure. Coughing. A sob. The nothingness of sleep.

Muso was gently shaken awake. A man's face—all candlelit golden and shadows, eyes dewy as if recently crying—hovered above him.

"I'm sorry to disturb you," he said in a whisper. "But I must let you know what is going on."

Muso, stiff and sore but feeling somewhat rejuvenated from the rest, sat up in his futon to give his full attention to this kind stranger who had saved him and welcomed him into his home.

"Early this morning, my father passed away," the man continued in hushed, nervous tones. "He was very ill and it was expected."

Muso expressed his condolences.

"Right before you arrived everyone had gathered to pay their respects." The man looked long behind him at the closed door.

"My apologies, but he is lying in repose in the next room."

"I, too, will offer my prayers," Muso said.

"It's not that." The man hissed, exasperated, through his teeth. Muso knew well that grief appeared in many forms. He didn't take offense at the sharp words.

"It took some time to wake you," he continued. "Everyone else has left. You see, we have a long tradition. When someone dies, the entire village spends the night in another community farther east. Please come with us. There is a place for you as well. We must leave now."

"But someone must stay and pray over your father." Muso didn't know what to make of this disrespectful custom.

"I know you are weary from your travels," the man said. "But strange things happen here after the death of a villager. If you are not afraid, you may stay and rest. We will return tomorrow morning."

"I am not afraid of anything," Muso said with a firm heart, completely forgetting the previous day's travails. "I will remain with your father and recite the necessary sutras to ease his soul into the next world."

"Thank you." The man backed away, bowed, then scrambled out the door.

Feeling confident he could pass the night watching over the deceased, Muso prepared himself and entered the next room. The body dressed in a white kimono lay with its head facing north as was the tradition. He shuffled over to close the front door that in his rush to leave, the nameless man left partially open.

Muso lit more incense and sat seiza next to the body. He noted the peaceful expression and thanked Buddha that his job tonight would be easy. Eyes open, unfocused on the lily pattern embroidered into the futon in front of him, hours passed as he rhythmically moved each sandalwood bead through his fingers and quietly chanted. The cadence of his deep voice along with the utter quiet of the room, the intoxicating fragrance of camphor smoke mixed with the sardine oil burning in the andon lamps, combined with the hum of physical exhaustion settled him in a meditative yet hyperaware state.

This lasted until his trance was interrupted by a sudden and disturbing realization. He was no longer alone in the room. He raised his gaze to see the front door thrown wide open. But when he tried to stand, a second and more harrowing revelation hit. His body was in the grips of kanashibari. Except for his eyes, he was completely frozen. *Fear arises and it fades away*, Muso told himself, trying to quash his panic. The platitude worked until something slid across the tatami mat to his left.

Muso tried desperately to turn his head, to raise his arms, to utter a prayer out loud. Nothing. The intruder took another dragging step closer. Lamp light shivered. Shadows whispered strangely along the floor and up the walls. Another rasping across the straw mat floor. Closer. The monk's throat tightened to that of a reed. Straight back, hands neatly in lap, he—like the great Buddha at

Nara—could only observe. Helpless. Closer. Something putrid watered his eyes. Then he saw it.

The monster stopped and crouched. Its breath rattled in its chest. Its long, emaciated limbs were bent and jutting at unnatural angles. It raised itself again, steadied the bloated belly and large malformed head by sinking clawed fingers into the tatami. There it hovered, staring directly down into the face of the deceased.

For as horrible as this was, Muso felt some relief. Whatever this fantastical abomination was, it didn't seem to notice him sitting like a statue just feet away. Maybe by some divine act Muso had been made invisible.

No sooner had he had the thought than the beast lifted that unholy head and looked right at him with its lead gray, almost human eyes. The monk's heart seized. Insects scurried across his skin. *This, too, is a delusion*, he repeated unconvincingly in his head. The monster held eye contact as it opened its mouth, widening it to reveal rows of needle-like teeth. It spat out a wormy tongue and licked the dead man's face. Then lengthening, it coiled around the corpse's neck. Still the mouth widened. With a sudden backward jerk of the head, the tongue tugged at the body, lifting it slightly.

No! Muso screamed in his thoughts and flailed his unmoving limbs. But there was nothing he could do but bear witness to the horrific scene. Another jerk and the man's entire head entered the maw. Little by little, the body was consumed, the awful tongue feeding the chomping teeth. The neck expanded to accommodate the meal, the stomach growing even larger, until Muso could take it no more and once again felt his world tilt and blackness descend.

He was shaken awake again by the same man as the night before. Only this time the room was lit by sunlight and Muso was lying exactly where he had fallen.

"It happened," the man said. "Are you okay?"

The monk pushed himself into a kneeling position and noting the absence of the dearly deceased, bowed in apology.

"We thought it might be different this time, with you here."

"I am sorry. I could not stop it."

Muso recounted what he'd seen and the man explained that this had been going on for generations, but how they were helpless to do anything about it. They had to feed it their dead.

"There is an old monk living in a hut near here. Why does he not perform the funeral rituals for you, why does he not come and expel this unholy monster? Have you not asked him?"

The son looked puzzled. "Yes, I know the place, but no one has lived there for many years."

Muso, shaken and confused, was also determined. He decided to return to the shack. That old sightless monk lived such a quiet, unobtrusive life the villagers hadn't even realized he was there. But it's a good thing he was. While the younger Muso lacked the confidence and experience to defeat it, together with the wiser, more learned man, they could save the valley people from this wretched, unholy beast. This, too, he reminded himself, as with everything in life, is a teaching from the Buddha.

In the light of day, the dilapidated abode looked worse than he remembered. No wonder the villagers thought it abandoned. Today the front door stood open. It was dark inside.

"Forgive my intrusion," Muso called out. "I know you wish to be alone. But I have come with an important favor to ask of you."

There was no reply. A shock of cold realization shook the young monk as he approached. Had yesterday been an illusion too? Had the old monk appeared just to guide him safely to the village below? Muso was confused. Suddenly he didn't know what was real and what wasn't. What was the lesson for him to learn in all of this? Muso was debating all this when the stench hit him. He hurried to the door and leaned inside.

"I'm sorry," crackled a voice from the shadows. "I am ashamed."

"My noble friend," Muso said, assuming the odor was just the inability of a weak, tottering old man to care for himself. "I can help you."

"Come in. Let me get the window."

Muso stepped inside and blinked in the gloom. The aged man banged on the wooden rain shutter to loosen it, then slid it open. Sunlight spilled into the tiny room, revealing the hellscape. Muso gasped. His walking stick clattered to the floor. Death was everywhere in piles of regurgitated bones, fur, flesh, and hair. He recognized the carcasses of monkeys, foxes, and tanuki all in various stages of mastication and decay scattered about and heaped up high in the corners. The most recent victim, though, identifiable by the soiled white kimono and what was left of a peaceful expression, the body from last night.

Muso swooned. No! His hand shot out and gripped the door frame. He steadied himself. No more running. His whole life his weak heart had gotten the better of him. Not today. A sprig of anger flared and gave him a burst of newfound strength. This was all an illusion. It was a test, a horror he must face. The young monk filled his lungs with the reek of death and rot. Face your fears. This was the teaching.

He watched the elderly monk step over what looked like the skeleton of a woman whose long hair was now brittle and dusty and tied in knots. He settled himself back on his filthy zabuton. He then looked around and began batting at the glittering dust motes that swam around his ugly, gore-crusted, sun-haloed head.

"You're not blind," Muso said.

"No." The senior monk turned to the younger one with sharp gray eyes. "I'm not."

Muso's legs turned to seaweed and he had to steel himself again against his softness.

"I'm a jikininki," the wicked beast continued. "A corpse eater. I was a monk once. Like you. Many, many years ago in a temple down in that very village." He pointed.

"I'm embarrassed now to say I was selfish and greedy and did not care at all for the lives or souls of the men and women I prayed over. I cared only about growing more wealthy, more powerful. This"—the venerable devil motioned to the carnage surrounding him—"Is my penance."

Muso examined the scene again, bile rising in his throat. This mirage was even more horrible than the night before.

"I do not enjoy this thing I have to do. I am sorry."

Something shifted. Muso sensed real regret in his voice and the look in the monster's eyes touched him. Anger and disgust softened to compassion and the urge to help.

"I will perform the segaki hungry ghost ritual on you," Muso said.

He lifted his robes and stepped carefully through the butchery, then gently used his sandaled feet to move aside another foul mound to clear a place for him to sit in front of the wretched fiend.

He pressed his hands together and prayed. He plunged down to tap the strength of the mountain itself and up into the infinite celestial space. After some moments he found his confidence. Soon his voice boomed a powerful staccato as the evil creature whimpered then wailed then writhed across the littered floor. Muso did not stop. Drunk on the powerful energy in the room, he went on, the firm word of the Buddha piercing the monster. Muso was not afraid.

But then as seemed to be his nature, or his karma, once a frenzy was reached, the walls began to spin and fall away, followed by the young monk collapsing once again into a dead faint.

When Muso came to this time, he was sprawled face down on a grassy patch of ground. Alone. The smell of dandelion and sweet clover danced him from his dreams. In the forest, songbirds chittered and called. His cheek was pleasantly wet with cool dew. Despite his awkward pose and disorientation, though, he felt rested.

The young monk rolled onto his back and stretched. He took a moment to gather his thoughts and admire the sky. The gold and red of dawn weren't yet burned off the clouds. It must be early. He wondered if the Buddha's paradise had clouds quite as lovely as these. Then he remembered.

The moments before he blacked out swam back. He sat up quickly and looked around. There stood the jikininki's hovel. But he was behind it now. No movement from the open window. Something else caught his attention. Muso crawled over to examine an old weathered gravestone. He ran his fingers over the moss-covered rock, scratched at it with fingernails, and read out loud the monk's name that had been chiseled there long ago. It was him. The old blind, well, not-blind monk. Had the ritual worked? Muso felt his knees growing damp and scrambled backwards. That's when he noticed the earth churned up at the foot of the grave. Maybe not as if something had left the grave, he told himself, but perhaps that something had crawled back in. Hope warmed his heart. Muso's prayers had worked.

He found his feet, uttered a final prayer, and located his walking stick. The tiny thought—maybe the turned earth was from the unspeakable beast crawling in and out of the grave—passed like a cloud through his mind.

Yes, there was no need to go any deeper into these hills. The coast of Enshu could wait for some other day. It was still early. If he hurried, he should be able to make it back home before any more beastly things came out.

Considered a very BAD omen
Accompanied by feelings of depression
Bright glowing eyes
Guardian of Gates to other realms
Sometimes associated with storms and/or strange weather
Often appears to be made of smoke

AFTERBURNER AND THE SHADOW OF BLACK DOG

Cindy O'Quinn

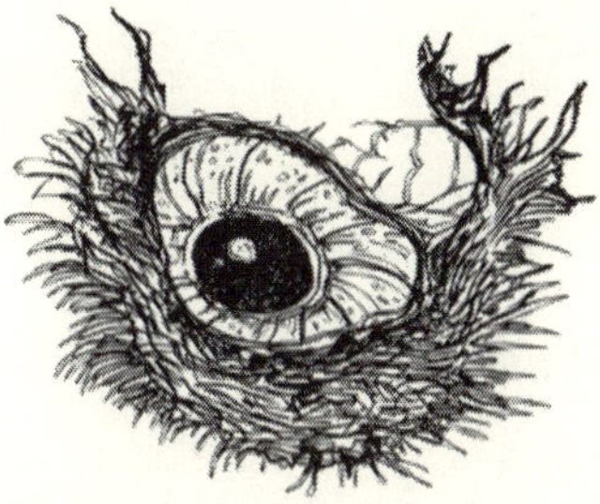

The first introduction …
I was inside my mother's belly, percolating.
Mom, Dad, and me. Made three.
The howls of the black dog equaled four.
Where were we for that first meeting?
The old church on the mountain. Glace.
Monroe County, West by God Virginia.
They were saved that day.
White Jesus in a dollar store, framed picture.
Kind eyes.
What did I know? I was in the womb, looking out.
Was I saved that day, as well?
Did they even know my seedling was present and
accounted for?
Saved by happenstance. Lucky me.

Second introduction …
Slapped on the ass, flicked on the foot.
I cried. Wouldn't you? The black dog growled.
Dad wanted a boy. Mom wanted a healthy baby.
The good doctor, well, he liked to have a little fun.
Downstairs of the two-story farmhouse/doctor's
office/delivery rooms,
he found my dad, pacing, waiting.

"Third one's the charm, Joe! You've got your boy."

I can only imagine the look on Dad's face. Pride.

By Mom's side, he looked at the bundle of pink joy.

"Little Joe." A smile from one ear to the next.

The look of confusion on Mom's face.

"Meet your daughter, Cynthia."

The good doctor was heard snickering in the hall.

Dad's face glowed red.
He called me Cindy.
Mom never did. I was Cynthia.
The black dog *stuck around.*

Life …
Five decades of memories.
Some good, some bad.
All stored in a memory box.

Deaths …
For there were many.
Some of us made tough, so we could survive
the suffering.
I didn't want to be tough.
I wanted to be one of the soft ones death didn't touch.
That wasn't my decision to make.
The black dog *preferred my company to others'.*
Like the good doctor, God had a way about him.
Babies, who didn't incubate quite long enough.
My sister who faded and couldn't stay.
A mother who smoked like a chimney every day.
Doped up driver took my dad's life away.

Afterburner …
You left me, and I didn't forgive you.
That place in my mind and heart where I carried the
pain.
Burned forever, nothing else to say.
Other than the black dog got its way.

Afterlife …
Where all my dead walk in light or dark.
Doesn't matter. I'm not there.
Pay me a visit sometime, I'm alone on this side.
No one said goodbye. That sucked!
Just up and died. No notes or reasons why.

"There you are. Will you stay with me for a while?
What do you mean, I'm on the other side now?"
But I left everyone behind. I didn't say goodbye.
There is no light. Before or after.

Only the night, worn as a disguise.
That's what awaits you in the afterlife.
Walking in darkness with your dead people.
And that damned black dog at my side.

MIDNIGHT MASS

F. Paul Wilson

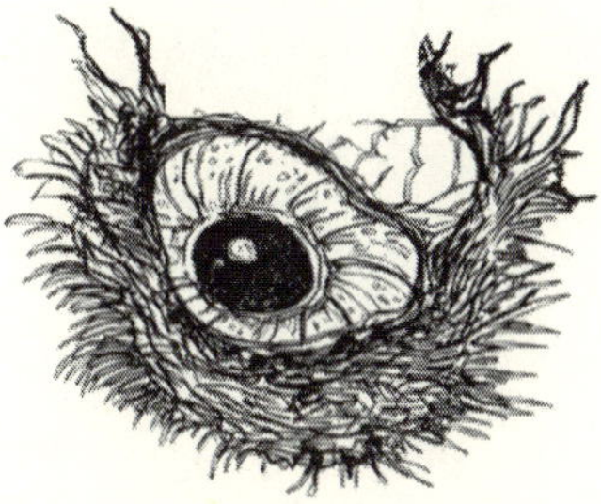

1

It had been almost a full minute since he'd slammed the brass knocker against the heavy oak door. That should have been proof enough. After all, wasn't the knocker in the shape of a cross? But no, they had to squint through their peephole and peer through the sidelights that framed the door.

Rabbi Zev Wolpin sighed and resigned himself to the scrutiny. He couldn't blame people for being cautious, but this seemed a bit overly so. The sun was in the west and shining full on his back; he was all but silhouetted in it. What more did they want?

I should maybe take off my clothes and dance naked?

He gave a mental shrug and savored the damp sea air. At least it was cool here. He'd bicycled from Lakewood, which was only ten miles inland from this same ocean but at least twenty degrees warmer. The bulk of the huge Tudor retreat house stood between him and the Atlantic, but the ocean's briny scent and rhythmic rumble were everywhere.

Spring Lake. An Irish Catholic seaside resort since before the turn of the century. He looked around at its carefully restored Victorian houses, the huge mansions arrayed here along the beach front, the smaller homes set in neat rows running straight back from the ocean. Many of them were still occupied. Not like Lakewood. Lakewood was an empty shell.

Not such a bad place for a retreat, he thought. He wondered how many houses like this the Catholic Church owned.

A series of clicks and clacks drew his attention back to the door as numerous bolts were pulled in rapid succession. The door swung inward, revealing a nervous-looking young man in a long black cassock. As he looked at Zev his mouth twisted and he rubbed the back of his wrist across it to hide a smile.

"And what should be so funny?" Zev asked.

"I'm sorry. It's just—"

"I know," Zev said, waving off any explanation as he glanced down at the wooden cross slung on a cord around his neck. "I know."

A bearded Jew in a baggy black serge suit wearing a yarmulke and a cross. Hilarious, no?

So, *nu?* This was what the times demanded, this was what it had come to if he wanted to survive. And Zev did want to survive. Someone had to live to carry on the traditions of the Talmud and the Torah, even if there were hardly any Jews left alive in the world.

Zev stood on the sunny porch, waiting. The priest watched him in silence.

Finally Zev said, "Well, may a wandering Jew come in?"

"I won't stop you," the priest said, "but surely you don't expect me to invite you."

Ah, yes. Another precaution. The vampire couldn't cross the threshold of a home unless he was invited in, so don't invite. A good habit to cultivate, he supposed.

He stepped inside and the priest immediately closed the door behind him, relatching all the locks one by one. When he turned around Zev held out his hand.

"Rabbi Zev Wolpin, Father. I thank you for allowing me in."

"Brother Christopher, sir," he said, smiling and shaking Zev's hand. His suspicions seemed to have been completely allayed. "I'm not a priest yet. We can't offer you much here, but—"

"Oh, I won't be staying long. I just came to talk to Father Joseph Cahill."

Brother Christopher frowned. "Father Cahill isn't here at the moment."

"When will he be back?"

"I … I'm not sure. You see—"

"Father Cahill is on another bender," said a stentorian voice behind Zev.

He turned to see an elderly priest facing him from the far end of the foyer. White-haired, heavyset, wearing a black cassock.

"I'm Rabbi Wolpin."

"Father Adams," the priest said, stepping forward and extending his hand.

As they shook, Zev said, "Did you say he was on 'another' bender? I never knew Father Cahill to be much of a drinker."

"Apparently there was a lot we never knew about Father Cahill," the priest said stiffly.

"If you're referring to that nastiness last year," Zev said, feeling the old anger rise in him, "I for one never believed it for a minute. I'm surprised anyone gave it the slightest credence."

"The veracity of the accusation was irrelevant in the final analysis. The damage to Father Cahill's reputation was a fait accompli.

Father Palmeri was forced to request his removal for the good of St. Anthony's parish."

Zev was sure that sort of attitude had something to do with Father Joe being on "another bender."

"Where can I find Father Cahill?"

"He's in town somewhere, I suppose, making a spectacle of himself. If there's any way you can talk some sense into him, please do. Not only is he killing himself with drink but he's become quite an embarrassment to the priesthood and to the Church."

Which bothers you more? Zev wanted to ask but held his tongue.

"I'll try."

He waited for Brother Christopher to undo all the locks, then stepped toward the sunlight.

"Try Morton's down on Seventy-One," the younger man whispered as Zev passed.

Zev rode his bicycle south on 71. It was almost strange to see people on the streets. Not many, but more than he'd ever see in Lakewood again. Yet he knew that as the vampires consolidated their grip on the world and infiltrated the Catholic communities, there'd be fewer and fewer day people here as well.

He thought he remembered passing a place named Morton's on his way to Spring Lake. And then up ahead he saw it, by the railroad track crossing, a white stucco one-story box of a building with "Morton's Liquors" painted in big black letters along the side.

Father Adams' words echoed back to him.

On another bender ...

Zev pushed his bicycle to the front door and tried the knob. Locked up tight. A look inside showed a litter of trash and empty shelves. The windows were barred; the back door was steel and locked as securely as the front. So where was Father Joe?

Then he spotted the basement window at ground level by the overflowing trash dumpster. It wasn't latched. Zev went down on his knees and pushed it open.

Cool, damp, musty air wafted against his face as he peered into the Stygian blackness. It occurred to him that he might be asking for trouble sticking his head inside, but he had to give it a try. If Father Cahill wasn't here, Zev would begin the return trek to Lakewood and write this whole trip off as wasted effort.

"Father Joe?" he called. "Father Cahill?"

"That you again, Chris?" said a slightly slurred voice. "Go home, will you? I'll be all right. I'll be back late."

"It's me, Joe. Zev. From Lakewood."

He heard shoes scraping on the floor and then a familiar face appeared in the shaft of light from the window.

"Well I'll be damned. It *is* you! Thought you were Brother Chris come to drag me back to the retreat house. Gets scared I'm gonna get stuck out after dark. So how ya doin', Reb? Glad to see you're still alive. Come on in!"

Zev saw that Father Cahill's eyes were glassy and he swayed ever so slightly, like a skyscraper in the wind. He wore faded jeans and a black Bruce Springsteen *Tunnel of Love Tour* sweatshirt. Zev's heart twisted at the sight of his friend in such condition. Such a mensch like Father Joe shouldn't be acting like a *shikker*. Maybe it was a mistake coming here. Zev didn't like seeing him like this.

"I don't have that much time, Joe. I came to tell you—"

"Get your bearded ass down here and have a drink or I'll come up and drag you down."

"All right," Zev said. "I'll come in but I won't have a drink."

He hid his bike behind the dumpster, then squeezed through the window. Father Joe helped him to the floor. They embraced, slapping each other on the back. Father Joe was a taller man, a giant from Zev's perspective. At six-four he was ten inches taller, at thirty-five he was a quarter-century younger; he had a muscular frame, thick brown hair, and on better days—clear blue eyes.

"You're grayer, Zev, and you've lost weight."

"Kosher food is not so easily come by these days."

"All kinds of food is getting scarce." He touched the cross slung from Zev's neck and smiled. "Nice touch. Goes well with your zizith."

Zev fingered the fringe protruding from under his shirt. Old habits didn't die easily.

"Actually, I've grown rather fond of it."

"So what can I pour you?" the priest said, waving an arm at the crates of liquor stacked around him. "My own private reserve. Name your poison."

"I don't want a drink."

"Come on, Reb. I've got some nice hundred-proof Stoly here. You've got to have at least *one* drink—"

"Why? Because you think maybe you shouldn't drink alone?"

Father Joe winced. "Ouch!"

"All right," Zev said. "*Bissel.* I'll have *one* drink on the condition that you *don't* have one. Because I wish to talk to you."

The priest considered that a moment, then reached for the vodka bottle.

"Deal."

He poured a generous amount into a paper cup and handed it over. Zev took a sip. He was not a drinker and when he did imbibe, he preferred his vodka ice cold from a freezer. But this was tasty. Father Cahill sat back on a crate of Jack Daniel's and folded his arms.

"*Nu?*" the priest said with a Jackie Mason shrug.

Zev had to laugh. "Joe, I still say that somewhere in your family tree is Jewish blood."

For a moment he felt light, almost happy. When was the last time he had laughed? Probably more than a year now, probably at their table near the back of Horovitz's deli, shortly before the St. Anthony's nastiness began, well before the vampires came.

Zev thought of the day they'd met. He'd been standing at the counter at Horovitz's waiting for Yussel to wrap up the stuffed derma he had ordered when this young giant walked in. He towered over the other rabbis in the place, looked as Irish as Paddy's pig, and wore a Roman collar. He said he'd heard this was the only place on the whole Jersey Shore where you could get a decent corned beef sandwich. He ordered one and cheerfully warned that it better be good. Yussel asked him what could he know about good corned beef and the priest replied that he grew up in Bensonhurst. Well, about half the people in Horovitz's on that day—and on any other day for that matter—grew up in Bensonhurst and before you knew it, they were all asking him if he knew such-and-such a store and so-and-so's deli.

Zev then informed the priest—with all due respect to Yussel Horovitz behind the counter—that the best corned beef sandwich in the world was to be had at Shmuel Rosenberg's Jerusalem Deli in Bensonhurst. Father Cahill said he'd been there and agreed one hundred per cent.

Yussel served him his sandwich then. As he took a huge bite out of the corned beef on rye, the normal *tummel* of a deli at lunchtime died away until Horovitz's was as quiet as a *shoul* on Sunday morning. Everyone watched him chew, watched him swallow. Then they waited. Suddenly his face broke into this big Irish grin.

"I'm afraid I'm going to have to change my vote," he said.

"Horovitz's of Lakewood makes the best corned beef sandwich in the world."

Amid cheers and warm laughter, Zev led Father Cahill to the rear table that would become theirs and sat with this canny and charming gentile who had so easily won over a roomful of strangers and provided such a *mechaieh* for Yussel. He learned that the young priest was the new assistant to Father Palmeri, the pastor at St. Anthony's Catholic church at the northern end of Lakewood. Father Palmeri had been there for years but Zev had never so much as seen his face. He asked Father Cahill—who wanted to be called Joe—about life in Brooklyn these days and they talked for an hour.

During the following months they would run into each other so often at Horovitz's that they decided to meet regularly for lunch, on Mondays and Thursdays. They did so for years, discussing religion—*Oy, the religious discussions!*—politics, economics, philosophy, life in general. During those lunchtimes they solved most of the world's problems. Zev was sure they'd have solved them all if the scandal at St. Anthony's hadn't resulted in Father Joe's removal from the parish.

But that was in another time, another world. The world before the vampires took over.

Zev shook his head as he considered the current state of Father Joe in the dusty basement of Morton's Liquors. "It's about the vampires, Joe," he said, taking another sip of the Stoly. "They've taken over St. Anthony's."

Father Joe snorted and shrugged.

"They're in the majority now, Zev, remember? They've taken over everything. Why should St. Anthony's be different from any other parish in the world?"

"I didn't mean the parish. I meant the church."

The priest's eyes widened slightly. "The church? They've taken over the building itself?"

"Every night," Zev said. "Every night they are there."

"That's a holy place. How do they manage that?"

"They've desecrated the altar, destroyed all the crosses. St. Anthony's is no longer a holy place."

"Too bad," Father Joe said, looking down and shaking his head sadly. "It was a fine old church." He looked up again, at Zev. "How do you know about what's going on at St. Anthony's? It's not exactly in your neighborhood."

"A neighborhood I don't exactly have any more."

Father Joe reached over and gripped his shoulder with a huge hand.

"I'm sorry, Zev. I heard how your people got hit pretty hard over there. Sitting ducks, huh? I'm really sorry."

Sitting ducks. An appropriate description. Oh, they'd been smart, those bloodsuckers. They knew their easiest targets. Whenever they swooped into an area, they singled out Jews as their first victims, and among Jews they picked the Orthodox first of the first. Smart. Where else would they be less likely to run up against a cross? It worked for them in Brooklyn, and so when they came south into New Jersey, spreading like a plague, they headed straight for the town with one of the largest collections of yeshivas in North America.

But after the Bensonhurst holocaust the people in the Lakewood communities did not take quite so long to figure out what was happening. The Reformed and Conservative synagogues started handing out crosses at Shabbes—too late for many but it saved a few. Did the Orthodox congregations follow suit? No. They hid in their homes and shules and yeshivas and read and prayed.

And were liquidated.

A cross, a crucifix—they held power over the vampires, drove them away. His fellow rabbis did not want to accept that simple fact because they could not face its devastating ramifications. To hold up a cross was to negate two thousand years of Jewish history, it was to say that the Messiah had come and they had missed him.

Did it say that? Zev didn't know. Argue about it later. Right now, people were dying. But the rabbis had to argue it now. And as they argued, their people were slaughtered like cattle.

How Zev railed at them, how he pleaded with them! Blind, stubborn fools! If a fire was consuming your house, would you refuse to throw water on it just because you'd always been taught not to believe in water? Zev had arrived at the rabbinical council wearing a cross and had been thrown out—literally sent hurtling through the front door. But at least he had managed to save a few of his own people. Too few.

He remembered his fellow Orthodox rabbis, though. All the ones who had refused to face the reality of the vampires' fear of crosses, who had forbidden their students and their congregations to wear crosses, who had watched those same students and congregations die en masse only to rise again and come for them. And soon those very same rabbis were roaming their own community, hunting the survivors, preying on other yeshivas, other congregations, until the entire community was liquidated and incorporated into the brotherhood of the vampire. The great fear had come to pass: they'd been assimilated.

The rabbis could have saved themselves, could have saved their people, but they would not bend to the reality of what was happening around them. Which, when Zev thought about it, was not at all out of character. Hadn't they spent generations learning to turn away from the rest of the world?

Those early days of anarchic slaughter were over. Now that the vampires held the ruling hand, the bloodletting had become more organized. But the damage to Zev's people had been done—and it was irreparable. Hitler would have been proud. His Nazi "final solution" was an afternoon picnic compared to the work of the vampires. They did in months what Hitler's Reich could not do in all the years of the Second World War.

There's only a few of us now. So few and so scattered. A final Diaspora.

For a moment Zev was almost overwhelmed by grief, but he pushed it down, locked it back into that place where he kept his sorrows and thought of how fortunate it was for his wife Chana that she died of natural causes before the horror began. Her soul had been too gentle to weather what had happened to their community.

"Not as sorry as I, Joe," Zev said, dragging himself back to the present. "But since my neighborhood is gone, and since I have hardly any friends left, I use the daylight hours to wander. So call me the Wandering Jew. And in my wanderings, I meet some of your old parishioners."

The priest's face hardened. His voice became acid.

"Do you, now? And how fares the remnant of my devoted flock?"

"They've lost all hope, Joe. They wish you were back."

He laughed. "Sure they do! Just like they rallied behind me when my name and honor were being dragged through the muck last year. Yeah, they want me back. I'll bet!"

"Such anger, Joe. It doesn't become you."

"Bullshit. That was the old Joe Cahill, naive turkey who believed all his faithful parishioners would back him up. But no. Palmeri tells the bishop the heat is getting too much for him, the bishop removes me, and the people I dedicated my life to all stand by in silence as I'm railroaded out of my parish."

"It's hard for the commonfolk to buck a bishop."

"Maybe. But I can't forget how they stood quietly by while I was stripped of my position, my dignity, my integrity, of everything I wanted to be …"

Zev thought Joe's voice was going to break. He was about to reach out to him when the priest coughed and squared his shoulders.

"Meanwhile, I'm a pariah over here in the retreat house, a goddam leper. Some of them actually believe—" He broke off in a growl. "Ah, what's the use? It's over and done. Most of the parish is dead anyway, I suppose. And if I'd stayed there, I'd probably be dead too. So maybe it worked out for the best. And who gives a shit anyway?"

He reached for the bottle of Glenlivet next to him.

"No-no!" Zev said. "You promised!"

Father Joe drew his hand back and folded his arms across his chest.

"Talk on, oh, bearded one. I'm listening."

Father Joe had certainly changed for the worse. Morose, bitter, apathetic, self-pitying. Zev was beginning to wonder how he could have called this man a friend.

"They've taken over your church, desecrated it. Each night they further defile it with butchery and blasphemy. Doesn't that mean anything to you?"

"It's Palmeri's parish. I've been benched. Let him take care of it."

"Father Palmeri is their leader."

"He should be. He's their pastor."

"No. He leads the vampires in the obscenities they perform in the church."

Father Joe stiffened and the glassiness cleared from his eyes.

"Palmeri? He's one of them?"

Zev nodded. "More than that. He's the local leader. He orchestrates their rituals."

Zev saw rage flare in the priest's eyes, saw his hands ball into fists, and for a moment he thought the old Father Joe was going to burst through.

Come on, Joe. Show me that old fire.

But then he slumped back onto the crate.

"Is that all you came to tell me?"

Zev hid his disappointment and nodded. "Yes."

"Good." He grabbed the scotch bottle. "Because I need a drink."

Zev wanted to leave, yet he had to stay, had to probe a little bit deeper and see how much of his old friend was left, and how much had been replaced by this new, bitter, alien Joe Cahill. Maybe there was still hope. So they talked on.

Suddenly he noticed it was dark.

"Gevalt!" Zev said. "I didn't notice the time!"

Father Joe seemed surprised too. He ran to the window and peered out.

"Damn! Sun's gone down!" He turned to Zev. "Lakewood's out of the question for you, Reb. Even the retreat house is too far to risk now. Looks like we're stuck here for the night."

"We'll be safe?"

He shrugged. "Why not? As far as I can tell I'm the only one who's been in here for months, and only in the daytime. Be pretty odd if one of those human leeches should decide to wander in here tonight."

"I hope so."

"Don't worry. We're okay if we don't attract attention. I've got a flashlight if we need it, but we're better off sitting here in the dark and shooting the breeze till sunrise." Father Joe smiled and picked up a huge silver cross, at least a foot in length, from atop one of the crates. Besides, we're armed. And frankly, I can think of worse places to spend the night."

He stepped over to the case of Glenlivet and opened a fresh bottle. His capacity for alcohol was enormous.

Zev could think of worse places too. In fact he had spent a

number of nights in much worse places since the holocaust. He decided to put the time to good use.

"So, Joe. Maybe I should tell you some more about what's happening in Lakewood."

After a few hours their talk died of fatigue. Father Joe gave Zev the flashlight to hold and stretched out across a couple of crates to sleep. Zev tried to get comfortable enough to doze but found sleep impossible. So he listened to his friend snore in the pitch darkness of the cellar.

Poor Joe. Such anger in the man. But more than that—hurt. He felt betrayed, wronged. And with good reason. But with everything falling apart as it was, the wrong done to him would never be righted. He should forget about it already and go on with his life, but apparently he couldn't. Such a shame. He needed something to pull him out of his funk. Zev had thought news of what had happened to his old parish might rouse him, but it seemed only to make him want to drink more. Father Joe Cahill, he feared, was a hopeless case.

Zev closed his eyes and tried to rest. It was hard to get comfortable with the cross dangling in front of him so he took it off but laid it within easy reach. He was drifting toward a doze when he heard a noise outside. By the dumpster. Metal on metal.

My bicycle!

He slipped to the floor and tiptoed over to where Father Joe slept. He shook his shoulder and whispered.

"Someone's found my bicycle!"

The priest snorted but remained sleeping. A louder clatter outside made Zev turn, and as he moved his elbow struck a bottle. He grabbed for it in the darkness but missed. The sound of smashing glass echoed through the basement like a cannon shot. As the odor of scotch whiskey replaced the musty ambiance, Zev listened for further sounds from outside. None came.

Maybe it had been an animal. He remembered how raccoons used to raid his garbage at home … when he'd had a home … when he'd had garbage …

Zev stepped to the window and looked out. Probably an animal. He pulled the window open a few inches and felt cool night air wash across his face. He pulled the flashlight from his coat pocket and aimed it through the opening.

Zev almost dropped the light as the beam illuminated a pale, snarling demonic face, baring its fangs and hissing. He fell back as the thing's head and shoulders lunged through the window, its curved fingers clawing at him, missing. Then it launched itself the rest of the way through, hurtling toward Zev.

He tried to dodge but he was too slow. The impact knocked the flashlight from his grasp and it went rolling across the floor. Zev cried out as he went down under the snarling thing. Its ferocity was overpowering, irresistible. It straddled him and lashed at him, batting his fending arms aside, its clawed fingers tearing at his collar to free his throat, stretching his neck to expose the vulnerable flesh, its foul breath gagging him as it bent its fangs toward him. Zev screamed out his helplessness.

2

Father Joe awoke to the cries of terror.

He shook his head to clear it and instantly regretted the move. His head weighed at least two hundred pounds, and his mouth was stuffed with foul-tasting cotton. Why did he keep doing this to himself? Not only did it leave him feeling lousy, it gave him bad dreams. Like now.

Another terrified shout, only a few feet away.

He looked toward the sound. In the faint light from the flashlight rolling across the floor he saw Zev on his back, fighting for his life against—

Damn! This was no dream! One of those bloodsuckers had got in here!

He leaped over to where the creature was lowering its fangs toward Zev's throat. He grabbed it by the back of the neck and lifted it clear of the floor. It was surprisingly heavy but that didn't slow him. Joe could feel the anger rising in him, surging into his muscles.

"Rotten piece of filth!"

He swung the vampire by its neck and let it fly against the cinderblock wall. It impacted with what should have been bone-crushing force but bounced off, rolled on the floor, and regained its feet in one motion, ready to attack again. Strong as he was, Joe knew he was no match for this thing's power. He turned, grabbed his big silver crucifix, and charged the creature.

"Hungry? Eat this!"

As the creature bared its fangs and hissed at him, Joe shoved the long lower end of the cross into its open mouth. Blue-white light flickered along the silver length of the crucifix, reflecting in the creature's startled, agonized eyes as its flesh sizzled and crackled. The vampire let out a strangled cry and tried to turn away but Joe wasn't through with it yet. He was literally seeing red as rage poured out of a hidden well and swirled through him. He rammed the cross deeper down the thing's gullet. Light flashed deep in its throat, illuminating the pale tissues from within. It tried to grab the cross and pull it out but the flesh of its fingers burned and smoked wherever they came in contact with it.

Finally, Joe stepped back and let the thing squirm and scrabble up the wall and out the window into the night. Then he turned to Zev. If anything had happened—

"Hey, Reb!" he said, kneeling beside the older man. "You all right?"

"Yes," Zev said, struggling to his feet. "Thanks to you."

Joe slumped onto a crate, momentarily weak as his rage dissipated. *This is not what I'm about*, he thought. But it had felt so damn good to let it loose on that vampire. Too good. And that worried him.

I'm falling apart ... like everything else in the world.

"That was too close," he said to Zev, giving the older man's shoulder a fond squeeze.

"Too close for that vampire for sure," Zev said, replacing his yarmulke. "And would you please remind me, Father Joe, that in the future if ever I should maybe get my blood sucked and become a vampire that I should stay far away from you."

Joe laughed for the first time in too long. It felt good.

They climbed out at first light. Joe stretched his cramped muscles in the fresh air while Zev checked on his hidden bicycle.

"Oy," Zev said as he pulled it from behind the dumpster. The front wheel had been bent so far out of shape that half the spokes were broken. "Look what he did. Looks like I'll be walking back to Lakewood."

But Joe was less interested in the bike than in the whereabouts of their visitor from last night. He knew it couldn't have got far. And it hadn't. They found the vampire—or rather what was left of it—on the far side of the dumpster: a rotting, twisted corpse, blackened to a crisp and steaming in the morning sunlight. The silver crucifix still protruded from between its teeth.

Joe approached and gingerly yanked his cross free of the foul remains.

"Looks like you've sucked your last pint of blood," he said and immediately felt foolish.

Who was he putting on the macho act for? Zev certainly wasn't going to buy it. Too out of character. But then, what *was* his character these days? He used to be a parish priest. Now he was a nothing. A less than nothing.

He straightened up and turned to Zev.

"Come on back to the retreat house, Reb. I'll buy you breakfast."

But as Joe turned and began walking away, Zev stayed and stared down at the corpse.

"They say they don't wander far from where they spent their lives," Zev said. "Which means it's unlikely this fellow was Jewish if he lived around here. Probably Catholic. Irish Catholic, I'd imagine."

Joe stopped and turned. He stared at his long shadow. The hazy rising sun at his back cast a huge hulking shape before him, with a dark cross in one shadow hand and a smudge of amber light where it poured through the unopened bottle of Scotch in the other.

"What are you getting at?" he said.

"The Kaddish would probably not be so appropriate so I'm just wondering if maybe someone should give him the last rites or whatever it is you people do when one of you dies."

"He wasn't one of us," Joe said, feeling the bitterness rise in him. "He wasn't even human."

"Ah, but he used to be before he was killed and became one of them. So maybe now he could use a little help."

Joe didn't like the way this was going. He sensed he was being maneuvered.

"He doesn't deserve it," he said, and knew in that instant he'd been trapped.

"I thought even the worst sinner deserved it," Zev said.

Joe knew when he was beaten. Zev was right. He shoved the cross and bottle into Zev's hands—a bit roughly, perhaps—then went and knelt by the twisted cadaver. He administered a form of the final sacrament. When he was through, he returned to Zev and snatched back his belongings.

"You're a better man than I am, Gunga Din," he said as he passed.

"You act as if they're responsible for what they do after they become vampires," Zev said as he hurried along beside him, panting as he matched Joe's pace.

"Aren't they?"

"No."

"You're sure of that?"

"Well, not exactly. But they certainly aren't human anymore, so maybe we shouldn't hold them accountable on human terms."

Zev's reasoning tone flashed Joe back to the conversations they used to have in Horovitz's deli.

"But Zev, we know there's some of the old personality left. I mean, they stay in their home towns, usually in the basements of their old houses. They go after people they knew when they were alive. They're not just dumb predators, Zev. They've got the old consciousness they had when they were alive. Why can't they rise above it? Why can't they … resist?"

"I don't know. To tell the truth, the question has never occurred to me. A fascinating concept: an undead refusing to feed. Leave it to Father Joe to come up with something like that. We should discuss this on the trip back to Lakewood."

Joe had to smile. So *that* was what this was all about.

"I'm not going back to Lakewood."

"Fine. Then we'll discuss it now. Maybe the urge to feed is too strong to overcome."

"Maybe. And maybe they just don't try hard enough."

"This is a hard line you're taking, my friend."

"I'm a hard-line kind of guy.'

"Well, you've become one."

Joe gave him a sharp look. "You don't know what I've become."

Zev shrugged. "Maybe true, maybe not. But do you truly think you'd be able to resist?"

"Damn straight."

Joe didn't know whether he was serious or not. Maybe he was just mentally preparing himself for the day when he might actually find himself in that situation.

"Interesting," Zev said as they climbed the front steps of the retreat house. "Well, I'd better be going. I've a long walk ahead of me. A long, *lonely* walk all the way back to Lakewood. A long, lonely, possibly *dangerous* walk back for a poor old man who—"

"All right, Zev! All *right!*" Joe said, biting back a laugh. "I get the point. You want me to go back to Lakewood. Why?"

"I just want the company," Zev said with pure innocence.

"No, really. What's going on in that Talmudic mind of yours? What are you cooking?"

"Nothing, Father Joe. Nothing at all."

Joe stared at him. Damn it all if his interest wasn't piqued. What was Zev up to? And what the hell? Why not go? He had nothing better to do.

"All right, Zev. You win. I'll come back to Lakewood with you. But just for today. Just to keep you company. And I'm not going anywhere near St. Anthony's, okay? Understood?"

"Understood, Joe. Perfectly understood."

"Good. Now wipe that smile off your face and we'll get something to eat."

3

Under the climbing sun they walked south along the deserted beach, barefooting through the wet sand at the edge of the surf. Zev had never done this. He liked the feel of the sand between his toes, the coolness of the water as it sloshed over his ankles.

"Know what day it is?" Father Joe said. He had his sneakers slung over his shoulder. "Believe it or not, it's the Fourth of July."

"Oh, yes. Your Independence Day. We never made much of secular holidays. Too many religious ones to observe. Why should I not believe it's this date?"

Father Joe shook his head in dismay. "This is Manasquan Beach. You know what this place used to look like on the Fourth before the vampires took over? Wall-to-wall bodies."

"Really? I guess maybe sunbathing is not the fad it used to be."

"Ah, Zev! Still the master of the understatement. I'll say one thing, though: the beach is cleaner than I've ever seen it. No beer cans or hypodermics." He pointed ahead. "But what's that up there?"

As they approached the spot, Zev saw a pair of naked bodies stretched out on the sand, one male, one female, both young and short-haired. Their skin was bronzed and glistened in the sun. The man lifted his head and stared at them. A blue crucifix was tattooed in the center of his forehead. He reached into the knapsack beside him and withdrew a huge, gleaming, nickel-plated revolver.

"Just keep walking," he said.

"Will do," Father Joe said. "Just passing through."

As they passed the couple, Zev noticed a similar tattoo on the girl's forehead. He noticed the rest of her too. He felt an almost-forgotten stirring deep inside him.

"A very popular tattoo," he said.

"Clever idea. That's one cross you can't drop or lose. Probably won't help you in the dark, but if there's a light on it might give you an edge."

They turned west and made their way inland, finding Route 70 and following it into Ocean County via the Brielle Bridge.

"I remember nightmare traffic jams right here every summer," Father Joe said as they trod the bridge's empty span. "Never thought I'd miss traffic jams."

They cut over to Route 88 and followed it all the way into Lakewood. Along the way they found a few people out and about in Bricktown and picking berries in Ocean County Park, but in the heart of Lakewood …

"A real ghost town," the priest said as they walked Forest Avenue's deserted length.

"Ghosts," Zev said, nodding sadly. It had been a long walk and he was tired. "Yes. Full of ghosts." In his mind's eye he saw the shades of his fallen brother rabbis and all the yeshiva students, beards, black suits, black hats, crisscrossing back and forth at a determined pace on weekdays, strolling with their wives on Shabbes, their children trailing behind like ducklings.

Gone. All gone. Victims of the vampires. Vampires themselves now, most of them. It made him sick at heart to think of those good, gentle men, women, and children curled up in their basements now to avoid the light of day, venturing out in the dark to feed on others, spreading the disease …

He fingered the cross slung from his neck. *If only they had listened!*

"I know a place near St. Anthony's where we can hide," he told the priest.

"You've traveled enough today, Reb. And I told you, I don't care about St Anthony's."

"Stay the night, Joe," Zev said, gripping the young priest's arm. He'd coaxed him this far; he couldn't let him get away now. "See what Father Palmeri's done."

"If he's one of them he's not a priest anymore. Don't call him *Father*."

"*They* still call him Father."

"Who?"

"The vampires."

Zev watched Father Joe's jaw muscles bunch.

Joe said, "Maybe I'll just take a quick trip over to St. Anthony's myself—"

"No. It's different here. The area is thick with them—maybe twenty times as many as in Spring Lake. They'll get you if your timing isn't just right. I'll take you."

"You need rest, pal."

Father Joe's expression showed genuine concern. Zev was detecting increasingly softer emotions in the man since their reunion last night. A good sign perhaps? "And rest I'll get when we get to where I'm taking you."

4

Father Joe Cahill watched the moon rise over his old church and wondered at the wisdom of coming back. The casual decision made this morning in the full light of day seemed reckless and foolhardy now at the approach of midnight.

But there was no turning back. He'd followed Zev to the second floor of this two-story office building across the street from St. Anthony's, and here they'd waited for dark. Must have been a law office once. The place had been vandalized, the windows broken, the furniture trashed, but there was an old Temple University Law School degree on the wall, and the couch was still in once piece. So while Zev caught some z's, Joe sat and sipped a little of his scotch and did some heavy thinking.

Mostly he thought about his drinking. He'd done too much of that lately, he knew; so much so that he was afraid to stop cold. So he was taking just a touch now, barely enough to take the edge off. He'd finish the rest later, after he came back from that church over there.

He'd stared at St. Anthony's since they'd arrived. It, too, had been extensively vandalized. Once it had been a beautiful little stone church, a miniature cathedral, really; very Gothic with all its pointed arches, steep roofs, crocketed spires, and multifoil stained glass windows. Now the windows were smashed, the crosses which had topped the steeple and each gable were gone, and anything resembling a cross in its granite exterior had been defaced beyond recognition.

As he'd known it would, the sight of St. Anthony's brought back memories of Gloria Sullivan, the young, pretty church volunteer whose husband worked for United Chemical International in New York, commuting in every day and trekking off overseas a little too often. Joe and Gloria had seen a lot of each other around the church offices and had become good friends. But Gloria had somehow got the idea that what they had went beyond friendship, so she showed up at the rectory one night when Joe was there alone. He tried to explain that as attractive as she was, she was not for him. He had taken certain vows and meant to stick by them. He did his best to let her down easy but she'd been hurt. And angry.

That might have been that, but then her six-year-old son Kevin had come home from altar boy practice with a story about a priest making him pull down his pants and touching him. Kevin was never clear on who the priest had been, but Gloria Sullivan was. Obviously it had been Father Cahill—any man who could turn down the heartfelt offer of her love and her body had to be either a queer or worse. And a child molester was worse.

She took it to the police and to the papers.

Joe groaned softly at the memory of how swiftly his life had become hell. But he had been determined to weather the storm, sure that the real culprit eventually would be revealed. He had no proof —still didn't—but if one of the priests at St. Anthony's was a pederast, he knew it wasn't him. That left Father Alberto Palmeri, St. Anthony's fifty-five-year-old pastor. Before Joe could get to the truth, however, Father Palmeri requested that Father Cahill be removed from the parish, and the bishop complied. Joe had left under a cloud that had followed him to the retreat house in the next county and hovered over him till this day. The only place he'd found even brief respite from the impotent anger and bitterness that roiled under his skin and soured his gut every minute of every day was in the bottle—and that was sure as hell a dead end.

So why had he agreed to come back here? To torture himself? Or to get a look at Palmeri and see how low he had sunk?

Maybe that was it. Maybe seeing Palmeri wallowing in his true element would give him the impetus to put the whole St. Anthony's incident behind him and rejoin what was left of the human race—which needed him now more than ever.

And maybe it wouldn't.

Getting back on track was a nice thought, but over the past few months Joe had found it increasingly difficult to give much of a damn about anyone or anything.

Except maybe Zev. He'd stuck by him through the worst of it, defending him to anyone who would listen. But an endorsement from an Orthodox rabbi had meant diddly in St. Anthony's. And yesterday Zev had biked all the way to Spring Lake to see him. Old Zev was all right.

And he'd been right about the number of vampires here too. Lakewood was *crawling* with the things. Fascinated and repelled, Joe had watched the streets fill with them shortly after sundown.

But what had disturbed him more were the creatures who'd come out *before* sundown.

The humans. Live ones.

The collaborators.

If there was anything lower, anything that deserved true death more than the vampires themselves, it was the still-living humans who worked for them.

Someone touched his shoulder and he jumped. It was Zev. He was holding something out to him. Joe took it and held it up in the moonlight: a tiny crescent moon dangling from a chain on a ring.

"What's this?"

"An earring. The local Vichy wear them."

"Vichy? Like the Vichy French?"

"Yes. Very good. I'm glad to see that you're not as culturally illiterate as the rest of your generation. Vichy humans—that's what I call the collaborators. These earrings identify them to the local nest of vampires. They are spared."

"Where'd you get them?"

Zev's face was hidden in the shadows. "Their previous owners … lost them. Put it on."

"My ear's not pierced."

A gnarled hand moved into the moonlight. Joe saw a long needle clasped between the thumb and index finger.

"That I can fix," Zev said.

"Maybe you shouldn't see this," Zev whispered as they crouched in the deep shadows on St. Anthony's western flank.

Joe squinted at him in the darkness, puzzled.

"You lay a guilt trip on me to get me here, now you're having second thoughts?"

"It is horrible like I can't tell you."

Joe thought about that. There was enough horror in the world outside St. Anthony's. What purpose did it serve to see what was going inside?

Because it used to be my church.

Even though he'd only been an associate pastor, never fully in charge, and even though he'd been unceremoniously yanked from the post, St. Anthony's had been his first parish. He was here. He might as well know what they were doing inside.

"Show me."

Zev led him to a pile of rubble under a smashed stained glass window. He pointed up to where faint light flickered from inside.

"Look in there."

"You're not coming?"

"Once was enough, thank you."

Joe climbed as carefully, as quietly as he could, all the while becoming increasingly aware of a growing stench like putrid, rotting meat. It was coming from inside, wafting through the broken window. Steeling himself, he straightened up and peered over the sill.

For a moment he was disoriented, like someone peering out the window of a city apartment and seeing the rolling hills of a Kansas farm. This could not be the interior of St. Anthony's.

In the flickering light of hundreds of sacramental candles he saw that the walls were bare, stripped of all their ornaments, of the plaques for the stations of the cross; the dark wood along the wall was scarred and gouged wherever there had been anything remotely resembling a cross. The floor, too, was mostly bare, the pews ripped from their neat rows and hacked to pieces, their splintered remains piled high at the rear under the choir balcony.

And the giant crucifix that had dominated the space behind the altar—only a portion of it remained. The crosspieces on each side had been sawn off and so now an armless, life-size Christ hung upside down against the rear wall of the sanctuary.

Joe took in all that in a flash, then his attention was drawn to the unholy congregation that peopled St. Anthony's this night. The collaborators—the Vichy humans, as Zev called them—made up the periphery of the group. They looked like normal, everyday people but each was wearing a crescent moon earring.

But the others, the group gathered in the sanctuary—Joe felt his hackles rise at the sight of them. They surrounded the altar in a tight knot. Their pale, bestial faces, bereft of the slightest trace of human warmth, compassion, or decency, were turned upward. His gorge rose when he saw the object of their rapt attention.

A naked teenage boy, his hands tied behind his back, was suspended over the altar by his ankles. He was sobbing and choking, his eyes wide and vacant with shock, his mind all but gone. The skin had been flayed from his forehead—apparently the Vichy had found an expedient solution to the cross tattoo—and blood ran in a slow stream across his abdomen and chest from his freshly truncated genitals. And beside him, standing atop the altar, a bloody-mouthed creature dressed in a long cassock. Joe recognized the thin shoulders, the graying hair trailing from the balding crown, but was shocked at the crimson vulpine grin he flashed to the things clustered below him.

"Now," said the creature in the lightly accented voice Joe had heard hundreds of times from St. Anthony's pulpit.

Father Alberto Palmeri.

And from the group a hand reached up with a straight razor and drew it across the boy's throat. As the blood flowed down over his face, those below squeezed and struggled forward like hatchling vultures to catch the falling drops and scarlet trickles in their open mouths.

Joe fell away from the window and vomited. He felt Zev grab his arm and lead him away. He was vaguely aware of crossing the street and heading toward the ruined legal office.

5

"Why in God's name did you want me to see that?"

Zev looked across the office toward the source of the words. He could see a vague outline where Father Joe sat on the floor, his back against the wall, the open bottle of scotch in his hand. The priest had taken one drink since their return, no more.

"I thought you should know what they were doing to your church."

"So you've said. But what's the reason behind that one?"

Zev shrugged in the darkness. "I'd heard you weren't doing well, that even before everything else began falling apart, you had already fallen apart. So when I felt it safe to get away, I came to see you. Just as I expected, I found a man who was angry at everything and letting it eat up his *guderim*. I thought maybe it would be good to give that man something very specific to be angry at."

"You bastard!" Father Joe whispered. "Who gave you the right?"

"Friendship gave me the right, Joe. I should hear that you are rotting away and do nothing? I have no congregation of my own anymore so I turned my attention on you. Always I was a somewhat meddlesome rabbi."

"Still are. Out to save my soul, ay?"

"We rabbis don't save souls. Guide them maybe, hopefully give them direction. But only you can save your soul, Joe."

Silence hung in the air for a while. Suddenly the crescent-moon earring Zev had given Father Joe landed in the puddle of moonlight on the floor between them.

"Why do they do it?" the priest said. "The Vichy—why do they collaborate?"

"The first were quite unwilling, believe me. They cooperated because their wives and children were held hostage by the vampires. But before too long the dregs of humanity began to slither out from under their rocks and offer their services in exchange for the immortality of vampirism."

"Why bother working for them? Why not just bare your throat to the nearest bloodsucker?"

"That's what I thought at first," Zev said. "But as I witnessed the Lakewood holocaust, I detected the vampires' pattern. They can choose who joins their ranks, so after they've fully infiltrated a population, they change their tactics. You see, they don't want too many of their kind concentrated in one area. It's like too many carnivores in one forest—when the herds of prey are wiped out, the predators starve. So they start to employ a different style of killing. For only when the vampire draws the life's blood from the throat with its fangs does the victim become one of them. Anyone drained as in the manner of that boy in the church tonight dies a true death. He's as dead now as someone run over by a truck. He will not rise tomorrow night."

"I get it," Father Joe said. "The Vichy trade their daylight services and dirty work to the vampires now for immortality later on."

"Correct."

There was no humor in the soft laugh the echoed across the room from Father Joe.

"Swell. I never cease to be amazed at our fellow human beings. Their capacity for good is exceeded only by their ability to debase themselves."

"Hopelessness does strange things, Joe. The vampires know that. So they rob us of hope. That's how they beat us. They transform our friends and neighbors and leaders into their own, leaving us feeling alone, completely cut off. Some can't take the despair and kill themselves."

"Hopelessness," Joe said. "A potent weapon."

After a long silence, Zev said, "So what are you going to do now, Father Joe?"

Another bitter laugh from across the room.

"I suppose this is the place where I declare that I've found new purpose in life and will now go forth into the world as a fearless vampire killer."

"Such a thing would be nice."

"Well screw that. I'm only going as far as across the street."

"To St. Anthony's?"

Zev saw Father Joe take a swig from the Scotch bottle and then screw the cap on tight.

"Yeah. To see if there's anything I can do over there."

"Father Palmeri and his nest might not like that."

"I told you, don't call him Father. And screw *him*. Nobody can do what he's done and get away with it. I'm taking my church back."

In the dark, behind his beard, Zev smiled.

6

Joe stayed up the rest of the night and let Zev sleep. The old guy needed his rest. Sleep would have been impossible for Joe anyway. He was too wired. He sat up and watched St. Anthony's.

They left before first light, dark shapes drifting out the front doors and down the stone steps like parishioners leaving a predawn service. Joe felt his back teeth grind as he scanned the group for Palmeri, but he couldn't make him out in the dimness. By the time the sun began to peek over the rooftops and through the trees to the east, the street outside was deserted.

He woke Zev and together they approached the church. The heavy oak and iron front doors, each forming half of a pointed arch, were closed. He pulled them open and fastened the hooks to keep them open. Then he walked through the vestibule and into the nave.

Even though he was ready for it, the stench backed him up a few steps. When his stomach settled, he forced himself ahead, treading a path between the two piles of shattered and splintered pews. Zev walked beside him, a handkerchief pressed over his mouth.

Last night, he had thought the place a shambles. He saw now that it was worse. The light of day poked into all the corners, revealing everything that had been hidden by the warm glow of the candles. Half a dozen rotting corpses hung from the ceiling—he hadn't noticed them last night—and others were sprawled on the floor against the walls. Some of the bodies were in pieces. Behind the chancel rail a headless female torso was draped over the front of the pulpit. To the left stood the statue of Mary. Someone had fitted her with foam rubber breasts and a huge dildo. And at the rear of the sanctuary was the armless Christ hanging head down on the upright of his cross.

"My church," he whispered as he moved along the path that had once been the center aisle, the aisle brides used to walk down with their fathers. "Look what they've done to my church!"

Joe approached the huge block of the altar. Once it had been backed against the far wall of the sanctuary, but he'd had it moved to the front so that he could celebrate Mass facing his parishioners. Solid Carrara marble, but you'd never know it now. So caked with dried blood, semen, and feces it could have been made of styrofoam.

His revulsion was fading, melting away in the growing heat of his rage, drawing the nausea with it. He had intended to clean up the place but there was so much to be done, too much for two men. It was hopeless.

"Fadda Joe?"

He spun at the sound of the strange voice. A thin figure stood uncertainly in the open doorway. A man of about fifty edged forward timidly.

"Fadda Joe, izat you?"

Joe recognized him now. Carl Edwards. A twitchy little man who used to help pass the collection basket at 10:30 Mass on Sundays. A transplantee from Jersey City—hardly anyone around here was originally from around here. His face was sunken, his eyes feverish as he stared at Joe.

"Yes, Carl. It's me."

"Oh, tank God!" He ran forward and dropped to his knees before Joe. He began to sob. "You come back! Tank God, you come back!"

Joe pulled him to his feet. “Come on now, Carl. Get a grip.”

“You come back ta save us, ain’tcha? God sent ya here to punish him, din’t He?”

“Punish whom?”

“Fadda Palmeri! He’s one a dem! He’s da woist a alla dem! He—”

“I know,” Joe said. “I know.”

“Oh, it’s so good to have ya back, Fadda Joe! We ain’t knowed what to do since da suckers took ova. We been prayin fa someone like youse an now ya here. It’s a freakin’ miracle!”

Joe wanted to ask Carl where he and all these people who seemed to think they needed him now had been when he was being railroaded out of the parish. But that was ancient history.

“Not a miracle, Carl,” Joe said, glancing at Zev. “Rabbi Wolpin brought me back.” As Carl and Zev shook hands, Joe said, “And I’m just passing through.”

“Passing t’rough? No. Dat can’t be! Ya gotta stay!”

Joe saw the light of hope fading in the little man’s eyes. Something twisted within him, tugging him.

“What can I do here, Carl? I’m just one man.”

“I’ll help! I’ll do whatever ya want! Jes tell me!”

“Will you help me clean up?”

Carl looked around and seemed to see the cadavers for the first time. He cringed and turned a few shades paler.

“Yeah … sure. Anyting.”

Joe looked at Zev. “Well? What do you think?”

Zev shrugged. “I should tell you what to do? My parish it’s not.”

“Not mine either.”

Zev jutted his beard at Carl. “I think maybe he’d tell you differently.”

Joe did a slow turn. The vaulted nave was utterly silent except for the buzzing of the flies around the cadavers. A massive clean-up job. But if they worked all day, they could make a decent dent in it. And then—

And then what?

Joe didn't know. He was playing this by ear. He'd wait and see what the night brought.

"Can you get us some food, Carl? I'd sell my soul for a cup of coffee."

Carl gave him a strange look.

"Just a figure of speech, Carl. We'll need some food if we're going to keep working."

The man's eyes lit again.

"Dat means ya staying?"

"For a while."

"I'll getcha some food," he said excitedly as he ran for the door. "An' coffee. I know someone who's still got coffee. She'll part wit' some of it for Fadda Joe." He stopped at the door and turned. "Ay, an' Fadda, I neva believed any a dem tings dat was said aboutcha. Neva."

Joe tried but he couldn't hold it back.

"It would have meant a lot to have heard that from you last year, Carl."

The man lowered his eyes. "Yeah. I guess it woulda. But I'll make it up to ya, Fadda. I will. You can take dat to da bank."

Then he was out the door and gone. Joe turned to Zev and saw the old man rolling up his sleeves.

"*Nu?*" Zev said. "The bodies. Before we do anything else, I think maybe we should move the bodies."

7

By early afternoon, Zev was exhausted. The heat and the heavy work had taken their toll. He had to stop and rest. He sat on the chancel rail and looked around. Nearly eight hours' work and they'd barely scratched the surface. But the place did look and smell better.

Removing the flyblown corpses and scattered body parts had been the worst of it. A foul, gut-roiling task that had taken most of the morning. They'd carried the corpses out to the small graveyard behind the church and left them there. Those people deserved a decent burial but there was no time for it today.

Once the corpses were gone, Father Joe had torn the defilements from the statue of Mary and then they'd turned their attention to the huge crucifix. It took a while but they finally found Christ's plaster arms in the pile of ruined pews. They'd been still nailed to the sawn-off cross-piece of the crucifix. While Zev and Father Joe worked at jury-rigging a series of braces to reattach the arms, Carl found a mop and bucket and began the long, slow process of washing the fouled floor of the nave.

Now the crucifix was intact again—the life-size plaster Jesus had his arms reattached and was once again nailed to his refurbished cross. Father Joe and Carl had restored him to his former position of dominance. The poor man was upright again, hanging over the center of the sanctuary in all his tortured splendor.

A grisly sight. Zev could never understand the Catholic attachment to these gruesome statues. But if the vampires loathed them, then Zev was for them all the way.

His stomach rumbled with hunger. At least they'd had a good breakfast. Carl had returned from his food run this morning with bread, cheese, and two thermoses of hot coffee. He wished now they'd saved some. Maybe there was a crust of bread left in the sack. He headed back to the vestibule to check and found an aluminum pot and a paper bag sitting by the door. The pot was full of beef stew and the sack contained three cans of Pepsi.

He poked his head out the doors but no one was in sight on the street outside. It had been that way all day—he'd spy a figure or two peeking in the front doors; they'd hover there for a moment as if to confirm that what they had heard was true, then they'd scurry away. He looked at the meal that had been left. A group of the locals must have donated from their hoard of canned stew and precious soft drinks to fix this. Zev was touched.

He called Father Joe and Carl.

"Tastes like Dinty Moore," Father Joe said around a mouthful of the stew.

"It is," Carl said. "I recognize da little potatoes. Da ladies of the parish must really be excited about youse comin' back to break inta deir canned goods like dis."

They were feasting in the sacristy, the small room off the sanctuary where the priests had kept their vestments—a clerical Green Room, so to speak. Zev found the stew palatable but much too salty. He wasn't about to complain, though.

"I don't believe I've ever had anything like this before."

"I'd be real surprised if you had," said Father Joe. "I doubt very much that something that calls itself Dinty Moore is kosher."

Zev smiled but inside he was suddenly filled with a great sadness. Kosher … How meaningless now seemed all the observances which he had allowed to rule and circumscribe his life. Such a fierce proponent of strict dietary laws he'd been in the days before the Lakewood holocaust. But those days were gone, just as the Lakewood community was gone. And Zev was a changed man. If he hadn't changed, if he were still observing, he couldn't sit here and sup with these two men. He'd have to be elsewhere, eating special classes of specially prepared foods off separate sets of dishes. But really, wasn't division what holding to the dietary laws in modern times was all about? They served a purpose beyond mere observance tradition. They placed another wall between observant Jews and outsiders, keeping them separate even from other Jews who didn't observe.

Zev forced himself to take a big bite of the stew. Time to break down all the walls between people … while there was still enough time and people left alive to make it matter.

"You okay, Zev?" Father Joe asked.

Zev nodded silently, afraid to speak for fear of sobbing. Despite all its anachronisms, he missed his life in the good old days of last year. Gone. It was all gone. The rich traditions, the culture, the friends, the prayers. He felt adrift—in time and in space. Nowhere was home.

"You sure?" The young priest seemed genuinely concerned.

"Yes, I'm okay. As okay as you could expect me to feel after spending the better part of the day repairing a crucifix and eating non-kosher food. And let me tell you, that's not so okay."

He put his bowl aside and straightened from his chair.

"Come on, already. Let's get back to work. There's much yet to do."

8

"Sun's almost down," Carl said.

Joe straightened from scrubbing the altar and stared west through one of the smashed windows. The sun was out of sight behind the houses there.

"You can go now, Carl," he said to the little man. "Thanks for your help."

"Where youse gonna go, Fadda?"

"I'll be staying right here."

Carl's prominent Adam's apple bobbed convulsively as he swallowed.

"Yeah? Well den, I'm staying too. I tol' ya I'd make it up ta ya, din't I? An besides, I don't tink the suckas'll like da new, improved St. Ant'ny's too much when dey come back tonight, d'you? I don't even tink dey'll get t'rough da doors."

Joe smiled at the man and looked around. Luckily it was July and the days were long. They'd had time to make a difference here. The floors were clean, the crucifix was restored and back in its proper position, as were most of the Stations of the Cross plaques. Zev had found them under the pews and had taken the ones not shattered beyond recognition and rehung them on the walls. Lots of new crosses littered those walls. Carl had found a hammer and nails and had made dozens of them from the remains of the pews.

"No. I don't think they'll like the new decor one bit. But there's something you can get us if you can, Carl. Guns. Pistols, rifles, shotguns, anything that shoots."

Carl nodded slowly. "I know a few guys who can help in dat department."

"And some wine. A little red wine if anybody's saved some."

"You got it."

He hurried off.

"You're planning Custer's last stand, maybe?" Zev said from where he was tacking the last of Carl's crude crosses to the east wall.

"More like the Alamo."

"Same result," Zev said with one of his shrugs.

Joe turned back to scrubbing the altar. He'd been at it for over an hour now. He was drenched with sweat and knew he smelled like a bear, but he couldn't stop until it was clean.

An hour later he was forced to give up. No use. It wouldn't come clean. The vampires must have done something to the blood and foulness to make the mixture seep into the surface of the marble like it had.

He sat on the floor with his back against the altar and rested. He didn't like resting because it gave him time to think. And when he started to think he realized that the odds were pretty high against his seeing tomorrow morning.

At least he'd die well fed. Their secret supplier had left them a dinner of fresh fried chicken by the front doors. Even the memory of it made his mouth water. Apparently, someone was *really* glad he was back.

To tell the truth, though, as miserable as he'd been, he wasn't ready to die. Not tonight, not any night. He wasn't looking for an Alamo or a Little Big Horn. All he wanted to do was hold off the vampires till dawn. Keep them out of St. Anthony's for one night. That was all. That would be a statement—*his* statement. If he found an opportunity to ram a stake through Palmeri's rotten heart, so much the better, but he wasn't counting on that. One night. Just to let them know they couldn't have their way everywhere with everybody whenever they felt like it. He had surprise on his side tonight, so maybe it would work. One night. Then he'd be on his way.

"What the fuck have you *done?*"

Joe looked up at the shout. A burly, long-haired man in jeans and a flannel shirt stood in the vestibule staring at the partially restored nave. As he approached, Joe noticed his crescent moon earring.

A Vichy.

Joe balled his fists but didn't move.

"Hey, I'm talking to you, mister. Are you responsible for this?"

When all he got from Joe was a cold stare, he turned to Zev.

"Hey, you! Jew! What the hell do you think *you're* doing?" He started toward Zev. "You get those fucking crosses off—"

"Touch him and I'll break you in half," Joe said in a low voice.

The Vichy skidded to a halt and stared at him.

"Hey, asshole! Are you crazy? Do you know what Father Palmeri will do to you when he arrives?"

"*Father* Palmeri? Why do you still call him that?"

"It's what he wants to be called. And he's going to call you *dog meat* when he gets here!"

Joe pulled himself to his feet and looked down at the Vichy. The man took two steps back. Suddenly he didn't seem so sure of himself.

"Tell him I'll be waiting. Tell him Father Cahill is back."

"You're a priest? You don't look like one."

"Shut up and listen. Tell him Father Joe Cahill is back—and he's pissed. Tell him that. Now get out of here while you still can."

The man turned and hurried out into the growing darkness. Joe turned to Zev and found him grinning through his beard.

"Father Joe Cahill is back—and he's pissed. I like that."

"We'll make it into a bumper sticker. Meanwhile let's close those doors. The criminal element is starting to wander in. I'll see if we can find some more candles. It's getting dark in here."

9

He wore the night like a tuxedo.

Dressed in a fresh cassock, Father Alberto Palmeri turned off County Line Road and strolled toward St. Anthony's. The night was lovely, especially when you owned it. And he owned the night in this area of Lakewood now. He loved the night. He felt at one with it, attuned to its harmonies and its discords. The darkness made him feel so alive. Strange to have to lose your life before you could really feel alive. But this was it. He'd found his niche, his metier.

Such a shame it had taken him so long. All those years trying to deny his appetites, trying to be a member of the other side, cursing himself when he allowed his appetites to win, as he had with increasing frequency toward the end of his mortal life. He should have given in to them completely long ago.

It had taken undeath to free him.

And to think he had been afraid of undeath, had cowered in fear each night in the cellar of the church, surrounded by crosses. Fortunately he had not been as safe as he'd thought and one of the beings he now called brother was able to slip in on him in the dark while he dozed. He saw now that he had lost nothing but his blood by that encounter.

And in trade he'd gained a world.

For now it was his world, at least this little corner of it, one in which he was completely free to indulge himself in any way he wished. Except for the blood. He had no choice about the blood. That was a new appetite, stronger than all the rest, one that would not be denied. But he did not mind the new appetite in the least. He'd found interesting ways to sate it.

Up ahead he spotted dear, defiled St. Anthony's. He wondered what his servants had prepared for him tonight. They were quite imaginative. They'd yet to bore him.

But as he drew nearer the church, Palmeri slowed. His skin prickled. The building had changed. Something was very wrong there, wrong inside. Something amiss with the light that beamed from the windows. This wasn't the old familiar candlelight, this was something else, something more. Something that made his insides tremble.

Figures raced up the street toward him. Live ones. His night vision picked out the earrings and familiar faces of some of his servants. As they neared, he sensed the warmth of the blood coursing just beneath their skins. The hunger rose in him and he fought the urge to rip into one of their throats. He couldn't allow himself that pleasure. He had to keep the servants dangling, keep them working for him and the nest. They needed the services of the indentured living to remove whatever obstacles the cattle might put in their way.

"Father! Father!" they cried.

He loved it when they called him Father, loved being one of the undead and dressing like one of the enemy.

"Yes, my children. What sort of victim do you have for us tonight?"

"No victim, Father—trouble!"

The edges of Palmeri's vision darkened with rage as he heard of the young priest and the Jew who had dared to try to turn St. Anthony's into a holy place again. When he heard the name of the priest, he nearly exploded.

"Cahill? Joseph Cahill is back in my church?"

"He was cleaning the altar!" one of the servants said.

Palmeri strode toward the church with the servants trailing behind. He knew that neither Cahill nor the Pope himself could clean that altar. Palmeri had desecrated it himself; he had learned how to do that when he became nest leader. But what else had the young pup dared to do?

Whatever it was, it would be undone. *Now!*

Palmeri strode up the steps and pulled the right door open—and screamed in agony.

The light! The *light!* The LIGHT! White agony lanced through Palmeri's eyes and seared his brain like two hot pokers. He retched and threw his arms across his face as he staggered back into the cool, comforting darkness.

It took a few minutes for the pain to drain off, for the nausea to pass, for vision to return.

He'd never understand it. He'd spent his entire life in the presence of crosses and crucifixes, surrounded by them. And yet as soon as he'd become undead, he was unable to bear the sight of one. As a matter of fact, since he'd become undead, he'd never even *seen* one. A cross was no longer an object. It was a light, a light so excruciatingly bright, so blazingly white that it was sheer agony to look at it. As a child in Naples he'd been told by his mother not to look at the sun, but when there'd been talk of an eclipse, he'd stared directly into its eye. The pain of looking at a cross was a hundred, no, a thousand times worse than that. And the bigger the cross or crucifix, the worse the pain.

He'd experienced monumental pain upon looking into St. Anthony's tonight. That could only mean that Joseph, that young bastard, had refurbished the giant crucifix. It was the only possible explanation.

He swung on his servants.

"Get in there! Get that crucifix down!"

"They've got guns!"

"Then get help. But get it *down!*"

"We'll get guns too! We can—"

"*No!* I want him! I want that priest alive! I want him for myself! Anyone who kills him will suffer a very painful, very long and lingering true death! Is that clear?"

It was clear. They scurried away without answering.

Palmeri went to gather the other members of the nest.

10

Dressed in a cassock and a surplice, Joe came out of the sacristy and approached the altar. He noticed Zev keeping watch at one of the windows. He didn't tell him how ridiculous he looked carrying the shotgun Carl had brought back. He held it so gingerly, like it was full of nitroglycerine and would explode if he jiggled it.

Zev turned, and smiled when he saw him.

"*Now* you look like the old Father Joe we all used to know."

Joe gave him a little bow and proceeded toward the altar.

All right. He had everything he needed. He had the Missal they'd found in among the pew debris earlier today. He had the wine; Carl had brought back about four ounces of sour red babarone. He'd found a smudged surplice and a dusty cassock on the floor of one of the closets in the sacristy, and he wore them now. No hosts, though. A crust of bread left over from breakfast would have to do. No chalice, either. If he'd known he was going to be saying Mass he'd have come prepared. As a last resort he'd used the can opener in the rectory to remove the top from one of the Pepsi cans from lunch. Quite a stretch from the gold chalice he'd used since his ordination, but probably more in line with what Jesus had used at that first Mass—the Last Supper.

He was uncomfortable with the idea of weapons in St. Anthony's but he saw no alternative. He and Zev knew nothing about guns, and Carl knew little more; they'd probably do more damage to themselves than to the Vichy if they tried to use them. But maybe the sight of them would make the Vichy hesitate, slow them down. All he needed was a little time here, enough to get to the consecration.

This is going to be the most unusual Mass in history, he thought.

But he was going to get through it if it killed him. And that was a real possibility. This might well be his last Mass. But he wasn't afraid. He was too excited to be afraid. He'd had a slug of the Scotch—just enough to ward off the DTs—but it had done nothing to quell the buzz of the adrenalin humming along every nerve in his body.

He spread everything out on the white tablecloth he'd taken from the rectory and used to cover the filthy altar. He looked at Carl.

"Ready?"

Carl nodded and stuck the .38 caliber pistol he'd been examining into his belt.

"Been a while, Fadda. We did it in Latin when I was a kid, but I tink I can swing it."

"Just do your best and don't worry about any mistakes."

Some Mass. A defiled altar, a crust for a host, a Pepsi can for a chalice, a fifty-year-old, pistol-packing altar boy, and a congregation consisting of a lone, shotgun-carrying Orthodox Jew.

Joe looked heavenward.

You do understand, don't you, Lord, that this was arranged on short notice?

Time to begin.

He read the Gospel but dispensed with the homily. He tried to remember the Mass as it used to be said, to fit in better with Carl's outdated responses. As he was starting the Offertory the front doors flew open and a group of men entered—ten of them, all with crescent moons dangling from their ears. Out of the corner of his eye he saw Zev move away from the window toward the altar, pointing his shotgun at them.

As soon as they entered the nave and got past the broken pews, the Vichy fanned out toward the sides. They began pulling down the Stations of the Cross, ripping Carl's makeshift crosses from the walls and tearing them apart. Carl looked up at Joe from where he knelt, his eyes questioning, his hand reaching for the pistol in his belt.

Joe shook his head and kept up with the Offertory.

When all the little crosses were down, the Vichy swarmed behind the altar. Joe chanced a quick glance over his shoulder and saw them begin their attack on the newly repaired crucifix.

"Zev!" Carl said in a low voice, cocking his head toward the Vichy. "Stop 'em!"

Zev worked the pump on the shotgun. The sound echoed through the church. Joe heard the activity behind him come to a sudden halt. He braced himself for the shot …

But it never came.

He looked at Zev. The old man met his gaze and sadly shook his head. He couldn't do it. To the accompaniment of the sound of renewed activity and derisive laughter behind him, Joe gave Zev a tiny nod of reassurance and understanding, then hurried the Mass toward the Consecration.

As he held the crust of bread aloft, he started at the sound of the life-sized crucifix crashing to the floor, cringed as he heard the freshly buttressed arms and crosspiece being torn away again.

As he held the wine aloft in the Pepsi can, the swaggering, grinning Vichy surrounded the altar and brazenly tore the cross from around his neck. Zev and Carl put up a struggle to keep theirs but were overpowered.

And then Joe's skin began to crawl as a new group entered the nave. There had to be at least forty of them, all of them vampires.

And Palmeri was leading them.

11

Palmeri hid his hesitancy as he approached the altar. The crucifix and its intolerable whiteness were gone, yet something was not right. Something repellent here, something that urged him to flee. What?

Perhaps it was just the residual effect of the crucifix and all the crosses they had used to line the walls. That had to be it. The unsettling aftertaste would fade as the night wore on. Oh, yes. His night brothers and sisters from the nest would see to that.

He focused his attention on the man behind the altar and laughed when he realized what he held in his hands.

"Pepsi, Joseph? You're trying to consecrate Pepsi?" He turned to his nest siblings. "Do you see this, my brothers and sisters? Is this the man we are to fear? And look who he has with him! An old Jew and a parish hanger-on!"

He heard their hissing laughter as they fanned out around him, sweeping toward the altar in a wide phalanx. The Jew and Carl—he recognized Carl and wondered how he'd avoided capture for so long—retreated to the other side of the altar where they flanked Joseph. And Joseph … Joseph's handsome Irish face so pale and drawn, his mouth set into a tight, grim line. He looked scared to death. And well he should be.

Palmeri put down his rage at Joseph's audacity. He was glad he had returned. He'd always hated the young priest for his easy manner with people, for the way the parishioners had flocked to him with their problems despite the fact that he had nowhere near the experience of their older and wiser pastor. But that was over now. That world was gone, replaced by a nightworld—Palmeri's world. And no one would be flocking to Father Joe for anything when Palmeri was through with him. "Father Joe"—how he'd hated it when way the parishioners had started calling him that. Well, their Father Joe would provide superior entertainment tonight. This was going to be *fun*.

"Joseph, Joseph, Joseph," he said as he stopped and smiled at the young priest across the altar. "This futile gesture is so typical of your arrogance."

But Joseph only stared back at him, his expression a mixture of defiance and repugnance. And that only fueled Palmeri's rage.

"Do I repel you, Joseph? Does my new form offend your precious shanty-Irish sensibilities? Does my undeath disgust you?"

"You managed to do all that while you were still alive, Alberto."

Palmeri allowed himself to smile. Joseph probably thought he was putting on a brave front, but the tremor in his voice betrayed his fear.

"Always good with the quick retort, weren't you, Joseph. Always thinking you were better than me, always putting yourself above me."

"Not much of a climb where a child molester is concerned."

Palmeri's anger mounted.

"So superior. So self-righteous. What about *your* appetites, Joseph? The secret ones? What are they? Do you always hold them in check? Are you so far above the rest of us that you never give in to an improper impulse? I'll bet you think that even if we made you one of us you could resist the blood hunger."

He saw by the startled look in Joseph's face that he had struck a nerve. He stepped closer, almost touching the altar.

"You do, don't you? You really think you could resist it! Well, we shall see about that, Joseph. By dawn you'll be drained—we'll each take a turn at you—and when the sun rises, you'll have to hide from its light. When the night comes, you'll be one of us. And then all rules will be off. The night will be yours. You'll be able to do anything and everything you've ever wanted. But the blood hunger will be on you too. You won't be sipping your god's blood, as you've done so often, but *human* blood. You'll thirst for hot, human blood, Joseph. And you'll have to sate that thirst. There'll be no choice. And I want to be there when you do, Joseph. I want to be there to laugh in your face as you suck up the crimson nectar, and keep on laughing every night as the red hunger lures you into infinity."

And it *would* happen. Palmeri knew it as sure as he felt his own thirst. He hungered for the moment when he could rub dear Joseph's face in the muck of his own despair.

"I was about to finish saying Mass," Joseph said coolly. "Do you mind if I finish?"

Palmeri couldn't help laughing this time.

"Did you really think this charade would work? Did you really think you could celebrate Mass on *this?*"

He reached out and snatched the tablecloth from the altar, sending the Missal and the piece of bread to the floor and exposing the fouled surface of the marble.

"Did you really think you could effect the Transubstantiation here? Do you really believe any of that garbage? That the bread and wine actually take on the substance of"—he tried to say the name but it wouldn't form—"the Son's body and blood?"

One of the nest brothers, Frederick, stepped forward and leaned over the altar, smiling.

"Transubstantiation?" he said in his most unctuous voice, pulling the Pepsi can from Joseph's hands. "Does that mean that this is the blood of the Son?"

A whisper of warning slithered through Palmeri's mind. Something about the can, something about the way he found it difficult to bring its outline into focus …

"Brother Frederick, maybe you should—"

Frederick's grin broadened. "I've always wanted to sup on the blood of a deity."

The nest members hissed their laughter as Frederick raised the can and drank.

Palmeri was jolted by the explosion of intolerable brightness that burst from Frederick's mouth. The inside of his skull glowed beneath his scalp and shafts of pure white light shot from his ears, nose, eyes—every orifice in his head. The glow spread as it flowed down through his throat and chest and into his abdominal cavity, silhouetting his ribs before melting through his skin. Frederick was liquefying where he stood, his flesh steaming, softening, running like glowing molten lava.

No! This couldn't be happening! Not now when he had Joseph in his grasp!

Then the can fell from Frederick's dissolving fingers and landed on the altar top. Its contents splashed across the fouled surface, releasing another detonation of brilliance, this one more devastating than the first. The glare spread rapidly, extending over the upper surface and running down the sides, moving like a living thing, engulfing the entire altar, making it glow like a corpuscle of fire torn from the heart of the sun itself.

And with the light came blast-furnace heat that drove Palmeri back, back, back until he had to turn and follow the rest of his nest in a mad, headlong rush from St. Anthony's into the cool, welcoming safety of the outer darkness.

12

As the vampires fled into the night, their Vichy toadies behind them, Zev stared in horrid fascination at the puddle of putrescence that was all that remained of the vampire Palmeri had called Frederick. He glanced at Carl and caught the look of dazed wonderment on his face. Zev touched the top of the altar—clean, shiny, every whorl of the marble surface clearly visible.

There was fearsome power here. Incalculable power. But instead of elating him, the realization only depressed him. How long had this been going on? Did it happen at every Mass? Why had he spent his entire life ignorant of this?

He turned to Father Joe.

"What happened?"

"I—I don't know."

"A miracle!" Carl said, running his palm over the altar top.

"A miracle and a meltdown," Father Joe said. He picked up the empty Pepsi can and looked into it. "You know, you go through the seminary, through your ordination, through countless Masses *believing* in the Transubstantiation. But after all these years … to actually *know*° ..."

Zev saw him rub his finger along the inside of the can and taste it. He grimaced.

"What's wrong?" Zev asked.

"Still tastes like sour barbarone … with a hint of Pepsi."

"Doesn't matter what it tastes like. As far as Palmeri and his friends are concerned, it's the real thing."

"No," said the priest with a small smile. "That's Coke."

And then they started laughing. It wasn't that funny, but Zev found himself roaring along with the other two. It was more a release of tension than anything else. His sides hurt. He had to lean against the altar to support himself.

It took the return of the Vichy to cure the laughter. They charged in carrying a heavy fire blanket. This time Father Joe did not stand by passively as they invaded his church. He stepped around the altar and met them head on.

He was great and terrible as he confronted them. His giant stature and raised fists cowed them for a few heartbeats. But then they must have remembered that they outnumbered him twelve to one and charged him. He swung a massive fist and caught the lead

Vichy square on the jaw. The blow lifted him off his feet and he landed against another. Both went down.

Zev dropped to one knee and reached for the shotgun. He would use it this time, he would shoot these vermin, he swore it!

But then someone landed on his back and drove him to the floor. As he tried to get up, he saw Father Joe, surrounded, swinging his fists, laying the Vichy out every time he connected. But there were too many. As the priest went down under the press of them, a heavy boot thudded against the side of Zev's head. He sank into darkness.

A throbbing in his head, stinging pain in his cheek, and a voice, sibilant yet harsh …

"Now, Joseph. Come on. Wake up. I don't want you to miss this!"

Palmeri's sallow features swam into view, hovering over him, grinning like a skull. Joe tried to move but found his wrists and arms tied. His right hand throbbed, felt twice its normal size; he must have broken it on a Vichy jaw. He lifted his head and saw that he was tied spread-eagle on the altar, and that the altar had been covered with the fire blanket.

"Melodramatic, I admit," Palmeri said, "but fitting, don't you think? I mean, you and I used to sacrifice our god symbolically here every weekday and multiple times on Sundays, so why shouldn't this serve as *your* sacrificial altar?"

Joe shut his eyes against a wave of nausea. This couldn't be happening.

"Thought you'd won, didn't you?" When Joe wouldn't answer him, Palmeri went on. "And even if you'd chased me out of here for good, what would you have accomplished? The world is ours now, Joseph. Feeders and cattle—that is the hierarchy. We are the feeders. And tonight you'll join us. But *he* won't. *Voila!*"

He stepped aside and made a flourish toward the balcony. Joe searched the dim, candlelit space of the nave, not sure what he was supposed to see. Then he picked out Zev's form and he groaned. The old man's feet were lashed to the balcony rail; he hung upside down, his reddened face and frightened eyes turned his way. Joe fell back and strained at the ropes but they wouldn't budge.

"Let him go!"

"What? And let all that good rich Jewish blood go to waste? Why, these people are the Chosen of God! They're a delicacy!"

"Bastard!"

If he could just get his hands on Palmeri, just for a minute.

"Tut-tut, Joseph. Not in the house of the Lord. The Jew should have been smart and run away like Carl."

Carl got away? Good. The poor guy would probably hate himself, call himself a coward the rest of his life, but he'd done what he could. Better to live on than get strung up like Zev.

We're even, Carl.

"But don't worry about your rabbi. None of us will lay a fang on him. He hasn't earned the right to join us. We'll use the razor to bleed him. And when he's dead, he'll be dead for keeps. But not you, Joseph. Oh no, not you." His smile broadened. "You're mine."

Joe wanted to spit in Palmeri's face—not so much as an act of defiance as to hide the waves of terror surging through him—but there was no saliva to be had in his parched mouth. The thought of being undead made him weak. To spend eternity like … he looked at the rapt faces of Palmeri's fellow vampires as they clustered under Zev's suspended form … like *them?*

He *wouldn't* be like them! He wouldn't allow it!

But what if there was no choice? What if becoming undead toppled a lifetime's worth of moral constraints, cut all the tethers on his human hungers, negated all his mortal concepts of how a life should be lived? Honor, justice, integrity, truth, decency, fairness, love—what if they became meaningless words instead of the footings for his life?

A thought struck him.

"A deal, Alberto," he said.

"You're hardly in a bargaining position, Joseph."

"I'm not? Answer me this: Do the undead ever kill each other? I mean, has one of them ever driven a stake through another's heart?"

"No. Of course not. "

"Are you sure? You'd better be sure before you go through with your plans tonight. Because if I'm forced to become one of you, I'll be crossing over with just one thought in mind: to find you. And when I do, I won't stake your heart, I'll stake your arms and legs to the pilings of the Point Pleasant boardwalk where you can watch the sun rise and feel it slowly crisp your skin to charcoal."

Palmeri's smile wavered. "Impossible. You'll be different. You'll want to thank me. You'll wonder why you ever resisted."

"You'd better sure of that, Alberto … for your sake. Because I'll have all eternity to track you down. And I'll find you, Alberto. I swear it on my own grave. Think on that."

"Do you think an empty threat is going to cow me?"

"We'll find out how empty it is, won't we? But here's the deal: let Zev go and I'll let you be."

"You care that much for an old Jew?"

"He's something you never knew in life, and never will know: He's a friend." *And he gave me back my soul.*

Palmeri leaned closer. His foul, nauseous breath wafted against Joe's face.

"A friend? How can you be friends with a dead man?" With that he straightened and turned toward the balcony. "Do him! *Now!*"

As Joe shouted out frantic pleas and protests, one of the vampires climbed up the rubble toward Zev. Zev did not struggle. Joe saw him close his eyes, waiting. As the vampire reached out with the straight razor, Joe bit back a sob of grief and rage and helplessness. He was about to squeeze his own eyes shut when he saw a flame arc through the air from one of the windows. It struck the floor with a crash of Glass and a *wooomp!* of exploding flame.

Joe had only heard of such things, but he immediately realized that he had just seen his first Molatov cocktail in action. The splattering gasoline caught the clothes of a nearby vampire who began running in circles, screaming as it beat at its flaming clothes. But its cries were drowned by the roar of other voices, a hundred or more. Joe looked around and saw people—men, women, teenagers—climbing in the windows, charging through the front doors. The women held crosses on high while the men wielded long wooden pikes—broom, rake, and shovel handles whittled to sharp points. Joe recognized most of the faces from the Sunday Masses he had said here for years.

St. Anthony's parishioners were back to reclaim their church.

"Yes!" he shouted, not sure of whether to laugh or cry. But when he saw the rage in Palmeri's face, he laughed. "Too bad, Alberto!"

Palmeri made a lunge at his throat but cringed away as a woman with an upheld crucifix and a man with a pike charged the altar—Carl and a woman Joe recognized as Mary O'Hare.

"Told ya I wun't letcha down, din't I, Fadda?" Carl said, grinning and pulling out a red Swiss Army knife. He began sawing at the rope around Joe's right wrist. "Din't I?"

"That you did, Carl. I don't think I've ever been so glad to see anyone in my entire life. But how—?"

"I told 'em. I run t'rough da parish, goin' house ta house. I told 'em dat Fadda Joe was in trouble an' dat we let him down before but we shoun't let him down again. He come back fa us, now we gotta go back fa him. Simple as dat. And den *dey* started runnin' house ta house, an' afore ya knowed it, we had ourselfs a little army. We come ta kick ass, Fadda, if you'll excuse da expression."

"Kick all the ass you can, Carl."

Joe glanced at Mary O'Hare's terror-glazed eyes as she swiveled around, looking this way and that; he saw how the crucifix trembled in her hand. She wasn't going to kick too much ass in her state, but she was *here*, dear God, she was here for him and for St. Anthony's despite the terror that so obviously filled her. His heart swelled with love for these people and pride in their courage.

As soon as his arms were free, Joe sat up and took the knife from Carl. As he sawed at his leg ropes, he looked around the church.

The oldest and youngest members of the parishioner army were stationed at the windows and doors where they held crosses aloft, cutting off the vampires' escape, while all across the nave—chaos. Screams, cries, and an occasional shot echoed through St. Anthony's. The vampires were outnumbered three to one and seemed blinded and confused by all the crosses around them. Despite their superhuman strength, it appeared that some were indeed getting their asses kicked. A number were already writhing on the floor, impaled on pikes. As Joe watched, he saw a pair of the women, crucifixes held before them, backing a vampire into a corner. As it cowered there with its arms across its face, one of the men charged in with a sharpened rake handle held like a lance and ran it through.

But a number of parishioners lay in inert, bloody heaps on the floor, proof that the vampires and the Vichy were claiming their share of victims too.

Joe freed his feet and hopped off the altar. He looked around for Palmeri—he *wanted* Palmeri—but the vampire priest had lost himself in the melee. Joe glanced up at the balcony and saw that Zev was still hanging there, struggling to free himself. He started across the nave to help him.

14

Zev hated that he should be hung up here like a salami in a deli window. He tried again to pull his upper body up far enough to reach his leg ropes but he couldn't get close. He had never been one for exercise; doing a sit-up flat on the floor would have been difficult, so what made him think he could do the equivalent maneuver hanging upside down by his feet? He dropped back, exhausted, and felt the blood rush to his head again. His vision swam, his ears pounded, he felt like the skin of his face was going to burst open. Much more of this and he'd have a stroke or worse maybe.

He watched the upside-down battle below and was glad to see the vampires getting the worst of it. These people—seeing Carl among them, Zev assumed they were part of St. Anthony's parish—were ferocious, almost savage in their attacks on the vampires. Months' worth of pent-up rage and fear was being released upon their tormentors in a single burst. It was almost frightening.

Suddenly he felt a hand on his foot. Someone was untying his knots. Thank you, Lord. Soon he would be on his feet again. As the cords came loose, he decided he should at least attempt to participate in his own rescue.

Once more, Zev thought. *Once more I'll try.*

With a grunt he levered himself up, straining, stretching to grasp something, anything. A hand came out of the darkness and he reached for it. But Zev's relief turned to horror when he felt the cold clamminess of the thing that clutched him, that pulled him up and over the balcony rail with inhuman strength. His bowels threatened to evacuate when Palmeri's grinning face loomed not six inches from his own.

"It's not over yet, Jew," he said softly, his foul breath clogging Zev's nose and throat. "Not by a long shot!"

He felt Palmeri's free hand ram into his belly and grip his belt at the buckle, then the other hand grabbed a handful of his shirt at the neck. Before he could struggle or cry out, he was lifted free of the floor and hoisted over the balcony rail.

And the dybbuk's voice was in his ear.

"Joseph called you a friend, Jew. Let's see if he really meant it."

15

Joe was halfway across the floor of the nave when he heard Palmeri's voice echo above the madness.

"Stop them, Joseph! Stop them now or I drop your friend!"

Joe looked up and froze. Palmeri stood at the balcony rail, leaning over it, his eyes averted from the nave and all its newly arrived crosses. At the end of his outstretched arms was Zev, suspended in mid-air over the splintered remains of the pews, over a particularly large and ragged spire of wood that pointed directly at the middle of Zev's back. Zev's frightened eyes were flashing between Joe and the giant spike below.

Around him Joe heard the sounds of the melee drop a notch, then drop another as all eyes were drawn to the tableau on the balcony.

"A human can die impaled on a wooden stake just as well as a vampire!" Palmeri cried. "And just as quickly if it goes through his heart. But it can take hours of agony if it rips through his gut."

St. Anthony's grew silent as the fighting stopped and each faction backed away to a different side of the church, leaving Joe alone in the middle.

"What do you want, Alberto?"

"First I want all those crosses put away so that I can see!"

Joe looked to his right where his parishioners stood.

"Put them away," he told them. When a murmur of dissent arose, he added, "Don't put them down, just out of sight. Please."

Slowly, one by one at first, then in groups, the crosses and crucifixes were placed behind backs or tucked out of sight within coats.

To his left, the vampires hissed their relief and the Vichy cheered. The sound was like hot needles being forced under Joe's fingernails. Above, Palmeri turned his face to Joe and smiled.

"That's better."

"What do you want?" Joe asked, knowing with a sick crawling in his gut exactly what the answer would be.

"A trade," Palmeri said.

"Me for him, I suppose'" Joe said.

Palmeri's smile broadened. "Of course."

"No, Joe!" Zev cried.

Palmeri shook the old man roughly. Joe heard him say, "Quiet, Jew, or I'll snap your spine!" Then he looked down at Joe again. "The other thing is to tell your rabble to let my people go." He laughed and shook Zev again. "Hear that, Jew? A Biblical reference —Old Testament, no less!"

"All right," Joe said without hesitation.

The parishioners on his right gasped in shock and cries of "No!" and "You can't" filled St. Anthony's. A particularly loud voice nearby shouted, "He's only a lousy kike!"

Joe wheeled on the man and recognized Gene Harrington, a carpenter. He jerked a thumb back over his shoulder at the vampires and their servants. "You sound like you'd be more at home with them, Gene."

Harrington backed up a step and looked at his feet.

"Sorry, Father," he said in a voice that hovered on the verge of a sob. "But we just got you back!"

"I'll be all right," Joe said softly.

And he meant it. Deep inside he had a feeling that he would

come through this, that if he could trade himself for Zev and face Palmeri one-on-one, he could come out the victor, or at least battle him to a draw. Now that he was no longer tied up like some sacrificial lamb, now that he was free, with full use of his arms and legs again, he could not imagine dying at the hands of the likes of Palmeri.

Besides, one of the parishioners had given him a tiny crucifix. He had it closed in the palm of his hand.

But he had to get Zev out of danger first. That above all else. He looked up at Palmeri.

"All right, Albert. I'm on my way up."

"Wait!" Palmeri said. "Someone search him."

Joe gritted his teeth as one of the Vichy, a blubbery, unwashed slob, came forward and searched his pockets. Joe thought he might get away with the crucifix but at the last moment he was made to open his hands. The Vichy grinned in Joe's face as he snatched the tiny cross from his palm and shoved it into his pocket.

"He's clean now!" the slob said and gave Joe a shove toward the vestibule.

Joe hesitated. He was walking into the snake pit unarmed. A glance at his parishioner' told him he couldn't very well turn back now.

He continued on his way, clenching and unclenching his tense, sweaty fists as he walked. He still had a chance of coming out of this alive. He was too angry to die. He prayed that when he got within reach of the ex-priest the smoldering rage at how he had framed him when he'd been pastor, at what he'd done to St. Anthony's since then would explode and give him the strength to tear Palmeri to pieces.

"No!" Zev shouted from above. "Forget about me! You've started something here and you've got to see it through!"

Joe ignored his friend.

"Coming, Alberto."

Father Joe's coming, Alberto. And he's pissed. Royally *pissed.*

16

Zev craned his neck around, watching Father Joe disappear beneath the balcony.

"Joe! Come back!"

Palmer shook him again.

"Give it up, old Jew. Joseph never listened to anyone and he's not listening to you. He still believes in faith and virtue and honesty, in the power of goodness and truth over what he perceives as evil. He'll come up here ready to sacrifice himself for you, yet sure in his heart that he's going to win in the end. But he's wrong."

"No!" Zev said.

But in his heart, he knew that Palmeri was right. How could Joe stand up against a creature with Palmeri's strength, who could hold Zev in the air like this for so long? Didn't his arms ever tire?

"Yes!" Palmeri hissed. "He's going to lose and we're going to win. We'll win for the same reason we'll always win. We don't let anything as silly and transient as sentiment stand in our way. If we'd been winning below and situations were reversed—if Joseph were holding one of my nest brothers over that wooden spike below—do you think I'd pause for a moment? For a second? Never! That's why this whole exercise by Joseph and these people is futile."

Futile, Zev thought. Like much of his life, it seemed. Like all of his future. Joe would die tonight and Zev would live on, a cross-wearing Jew, with the traditions of his past sacked and in flames, and nothing in his future but a vast, empty, limitless plain to wander alone.

There was a sound on the balcony stairs and Palmer turned his head.

"Ah, Joseph," he said.

Zev couldn't see the priest but he shouted anyway.

"Go back Joe! Don't let him trick you!"

"Speaking of tricks," Palmeri said, leaning further over the balcony rail as an extra warning to Joe, "I hope you're not going to try anything foolish."

"No," said Joe's tired voice from somewhere behind Palmeri. "No tricks. Pull him in and let him go."

Zev could not let this happen. And suddenly he knew what he had to do. He twisted his body and grabbed the front of Palmeri's cassock while bringing his legs up and bracing his feet against one of the uprights of the brass balcony rail. As Palmeri turned his startled face toward him, Zev put all his strength into his legs for one convulsive backwards push against the railing, pulling Palmeri with him. The vampire priest was overbalanced. Even his enormous strength could not help him once his feet came free of the floor. Zev saw his undead eyes widen with terror as his lower body slipped over the railing. As they fell free, Zev wrapped his arms around Palmeri and clutched his cold and surprisingly thin body tightly against him.

"What goes through this old Jew goes through you!" he shouted into the vampire's ear.

For an instant he saw Joe's horrified face appear over the balcony's receding edge, heard Joe's faraway shout of "*No!*" mingle with Palmeri's nearer scream of the same word, then there was a spine-cracking jar and a tearing, wrenching pain beyond all comprehension in his chest. In an eyeblink he felt the sharp spire of wood rip through him and into Palmeri.

And then he felt no more.

As roaring blackness closed in, he wondered if he'd done it, if this last desperate, foolish act had succeeded. He didn't want to die without finding out. He wanted to know—

But then he knew no more.

17

Joe shouted incoherently as he hung over the rail and watched Zev's fall, gagged as he saw the bloody point of the pew remnant burst through the back of Palmeri's cassock directly below him. He saw Palmeri squirm and flop around like a speared fish, then go limp atop Zev's already inert form.

As cheers mixed with cries of horror and the sounds of renewed battle rose from the nave, Joe turned away from the balcony rail and dropped to his knees.

"Zev!" he cried aloud. "Good God, Zev!"

Forcing himself to his feet, he stumbled down the back stairs, through the vestibule. and into the nave. The vampires and the Vichy were on the run, as cowed and demoralized by their leader's death as the parishioners were buoyed by it. Slowly, steadily, they were falling before the relentless onslaught. But Joe paid them scant attention. He fought his way to where Zev lay impaled beneath Palmeri's already rotting corpse. He looked for a sign of life in his old friend's glazing eyes, a hint of a pulse in his throat under his beard, but there was nothing.

"Oh, Zev, you shouldn't have. You shouldn't have."

Suddenly he was surrounded by a cheering throng of St. Anthony's parishioners.

"We did it, Fadda Joe!" Carl cried, his face and hands splattered with blood. "We killed 'em all! We got our church back!"

"Thanks to this man here," Joe said, pointing to Zev.

"No" someone shouted. "Thanks to *you!*"

Amid the cheers, Joe shook his head and said nothing. Let them celebrate. They deserved it. They'd reclaimed a small piece of the planet as their own, a toehold and nothing more. A small victory of minimal significance in the war, but a victory nonetheless. They had their church back, at least for tonight. And they intended to keep it.

Good. But there would be one change. If they wanted their Father Joe to stick around, they were going to have to agree to rename the church.

St. Zev's.

Joe liked the sound of that.

NIGHT HUNGER

Stephanie Ellis

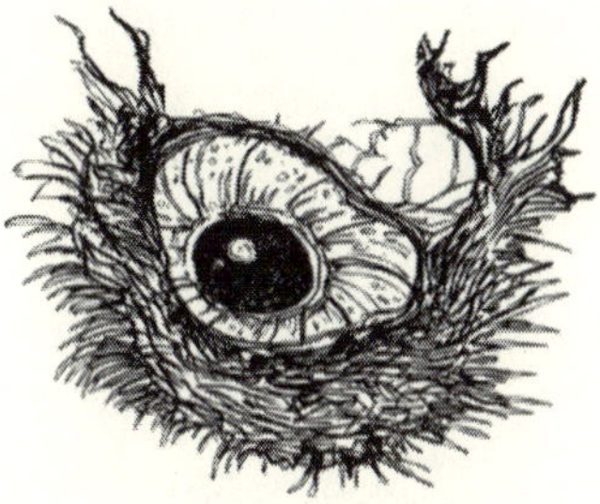

The corpse road is my road,
path mapped by Hell
to haunt travellers,
snare the unwary
feed the fires
of her hall of hate

but she is gone

bequeathing me her knife
of famine, the craving
for touch and taste
of human flesh
which I am free to fill
at my leisure

This night, the moon
hides its eye
prefers not to watch
me walk, stalk
the land
curl my claws around
an innocent neck
break bone and body and hope,
though still not enough to sate desire

Driven, I look for the shape
of another Adam,
another Eve,

and I open my arms
in welcome.

Undead Golem
in the form of a
scarecrow
Traditional Materials
used
as well
as
human
bones
Created
by a
Lonely
Farmer
Nocturnal
Powered by
the maker's emotions +
desires

THE COMPANION

Joe R. Lansdale, Kasey Jo Lansdale
and Keith Lansdale

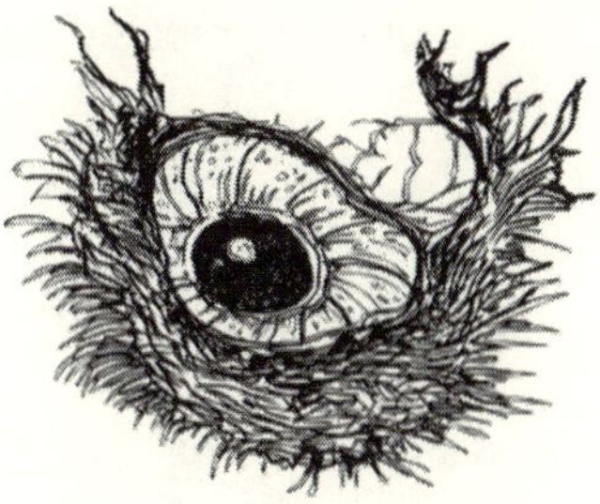

They weren't biting.

Harold sat on the bank with his fishing pole and watched the clear creek water turn dark as the sunlight faded. He knew he should pack up and go. This wonderful fishing spot he'd heard about was a dud, but the idea of going home without at least one fish for supper was not a happy one. He had spent a large part of the day before bragging to his friends about what a fisherman he was. He could hear them now, laughing and joking as he talked about the big one that got away.

And worse yet, he was out of bait.

He had used his little camp shovel to dig around the edge of the bank for worms. But he hadn't turned up so much as a grub or a doodlebug.

The best course of action, other than pack his gear on his bike and ride home, was to cross the bank. It was less wooded over there, and the ground might be softer. On the other side of the creek, through a thinning row of trees, he could see an old farm field. There were dried stalks of broken-down corn and tall dried weeds the plain brown color of a cardboard box.

Harold looked at his watch. He decided he had just enough time to find some bait and maybe catch one fish. He picked up his camp shovel and found a narrow place in the creek to leap across. After walking through the trees and out into the huge field, he noticed a large and odd-looking scarecrow on a post. Beyond the scarecrow, some stretch away, surrounded by saplings and weeds, he saw what had once been a fine two-story farmhouse. Now it was not much more than an abandoned shell of broken glass and aging lumber.

As Harold approached the scarecrow, he was even more taken with its unusual appearance. It was dressed in a stovepipe hat that was crunched and moth-eaten and leaned to one side. The body was constructed of hay, sticks, and vines, and the face was made of some sort of cloth, perhaps an old tow sack. It was dressed in a once expensive evening jacket and pants. Its arms were outstretched on a pole, and poking out of its sleeves were fingers made of sticks.

From a distance, the eyes looked like empty sockets in a skull. When Harold stood close to the scarecrow, he was even more surprised to discover it had teeth. They were animal teeth, still in the jawbone, and someone had fitted them into the cloth face, giving the scarecrow a wolf-like countenance. Dark feathers had somehow gotten caught between the teeth.

But the most peculiar thing of all was found at the center of the scarecrow. Its black jacket hung open, its chest was torn apart, and Harold could see inside. He was startled to discover that there was a rib cage, and fastened to it by a cord was a large, faded valentine heart. A long, thick stick was rammed directly through that heart.

The dirt beneath the scarecrow was soft, and Harold took his shovel and began to dig. As he did, he had a sensation of being watched. Then he saw a shadow, as if the scarecrow were nodding its head.

Harold glanced up and saw that the shadow was made by a large crow flying high overhead. The early rising moon had caught its shape and cast it on the ground. This gave Harold a sense of relief, but he realized that any plans to continue fishing were wasted. It was too late.

A grunting noise behind him caused him to jump up, leaving his camp shovel in the dirt. He grabbed at the first weapon he saw—the stick jammed through the scarecrow. He jerked it free and saw the source of the noise—a wild East Texas boar. A dangerous animal indeed.

It was a big one. Black and angry-looking, with eyes that caught the moonlight and burned back at him like coals. The beast's tusks shone like wet knives, and Harold knew those tusks could tear him apart as easily as he might rip wet construction paper with his hands.

The boar turned its head from side to side and snorted, taking in the boy's smell. Harold tried to maintain his ground. But then the moonlight shifted in the boar's eyes and made them seem even brighter than before. Harold panicked and began running toward the farmhouse.

He heard the boar running behind him. It sounded strange as it came, as if it were chasing him on padded feet. Harold reached the front door of the farmhouse and grabbed the door handle. In one swift motion, he swung inside and pushed it shut. The boar rammed the door, and the house rattled like dry bones.

The door had a bar lock, and Harold pushed it into place. He leaped back, holding the stick to use as a spear. The ramming continued for a moment, then everything went quiet.

Harold eased to a window and looked out. The boar was standing at the edge of the woods near where he had first seen it.

The scarecrow was gone, and in its place there was only the post that had held it.

Harold was confused. How had the boar chased him to the house and returned to its original position so quickly? And what had happened to the scarecrow? Had the boar, thinking the scarecrow was a person, torn it from the post with its tusks?

The boar turned and disappeared into the woods. Harold decided to give the animal time to get far away. He checked his watch, then waited a few minutes. While he waited, he looked around.

The house was a wreck. There were overturned chairs, a table, and books. Near the fireplace, a hatchet was stuck in a large log. Everything was coated in dust and spiderwebs, and the stairs that twisted up to the second landing were shaky and rotten.

Harold was about to return to his fishing gear and head for the bike when he heard a scraping noise. He wheeled around for a look. The wind was moving a clutch of weeds, causing them to scrape against the window. Harold felt like a fool. Everything was scaring him.

Then the weeds moved from view and he discovered they weren't weeds at all. In fact, they looked like sticks … or fingers.

Hadn't the scarecrow had sticks for fingers?

That was ridiculous. Scarecrows didn't move on their own.

Then again, Harold thought as he looked out the window at the scarecrow's post, *where was it?*

The doorknob turned slowly. The door moved slightly, but the bar lock held. Harold could feel the hair on the back of his neck bristling. Goosebumps moved along his neck and shoulders.

The knob turned again.

Then something pushed hard against the door. Harder.

Harold dropped the stick and wrenched the hatchet from the log.

At the bottom of the door was a space about an inch wide, and the moonlight shining through the windows made it possible for him to see something scuttling there—sticks, long and flexible.

They poked through the crack at the bottom of the door, tapped loudly on the floor, and stretched, stretched, stretched farther into the room. A flat hand made of hay, vines, and sticks appeared. It began to ascend on the end of a knotty vine of an arm, wiggling its fingers as it rose. It climbed along the door, and Harold realized, to his horror and astonishment, that it was trying to reach the bar lock.

Harold stood frozen, watching the fingers push and free the latch.

Harold came unfrozen long enough to leap forward and chop down on the knotty elbow, striking it in two. The hand flopped to the floor and clutched so hard at the floorboards that it scratched large strips of wood from them. Then it was still.

But Harold had moved too late. The doorknob was turning again. Harold darted for the stairway, bolted up the staircase. Behind him came a scuttling sound. He was almost to the top of the stairs when the step beneath him gave way and his foot went through with a screech of nails and a crash of rotten lumber.

Harold let out a scream as something grabbed hold of the back of his coat collar. He jerked loose, tearing his jacket and losing the hatchet in the process. He tugged his foot free and crawled rapidly on hands and knees to the top of the stairs.

He struggled to his feet and raced down the corridor. Moonlight shone through a hall window and projected his shadow and that of his capering pursuer onto the wall. Then the creature sprang onto Harold's back, sending both of them tumbling to the floor.

They rolled and twisted down the hallway. Harold howled and clutched at the strong arm wrapped around his throat. As he turned over onto his back, he heard the crunching of sticks beneath him. The arm loosened its grip, and Harold was able to free himself. He scuttled along the floor like a cockroach, regained his footing, then darted through an open door and slammed it.

Out in the hall he heard it moving. Sticks crackled. Hay swished. The thing was coming after him.

Harold checked over his shoulder, trying to find something to jam against the door, or some place to hide. He saw another doorway and sprinted for that. It led to another hall, and down its length was a series of doors. Harold quickly entered the room at the far end and closed the door quietly. He fumbled for a lock but there was none. He saw a bed and rolled under it, sliding up against the wall where it was darkest.

The moon was rising, and its light was inching under the bed. Dust particles swam in the moonlight. The ancient bed smelled musty and wet. Outside in the hall, Harold could hear the thing scooting along as if it were sweeping the floor. Scooting closer.

A door opened. Closed.

A little later another door opened and closed.

Then another.

Moments later he could hear it in the room next to his. He knew he should try to escape, but to where? He was trapped. If he tried to rush out the door, he was certain to run right into it. Shivering like a frightened kitten, he pushed himself farther up against the wall, as close as possible.

The bedroom door creaked open. The scarecrow shuffled into the room. Harold could hear it moving from one side to the other, pulling things from shelves, tossing them onto the floor, smashing glass, trying to find his hiding place.

Please, please, thought Harold, *don't look under the bed.*

Harold heard it brushing toward the door, then he heard the door open. *It's going to leave,* thought Harold. *It's going to leave!*

But it stopped. Then slowly turned and walked to the bed. Harold could see the scarecrow's straw-filled pants legs, its shapeless straw feet. Bits of hay floated down from the scarecrow, coasted under the bed and lay in the moonlight, just inches away.

Slowly the scarecrow bent down for a look. The shadow of its hat poked beneath the bed before its actual face. Harold couldn't stand to look. He felt as if he might scream. The beating of his heart seemed as loud as thunder.

It looked under the bed.

Harold, eyes closed, waited for it to grab him.

Seconds ticked by and nothing happened.

Harold snapped his eyes open to the sound of the door slamming.

It hadn't seen him.

The thick shadows closest to the wall had protected him. If it had been a few minutes later, the rising moonlight would have expanded under the bed and revealed him.

Harold lay there, trying to decide what to do. Strangely enough, he felt sleepy. He couldn't imagine how that could be, but finally he decided that a mind could only take so much terror before it needed relief—even if it was false relief. He closed his eyes and fell into a deep sleep.

When he awoke, he realized by the light in the room that it was near sunrise. He had slept for hours. He wondered if the scarecrow was still in the house, searching.

Building his nerve, Harold crawled from under the bed. He stretched his back and turned to look around the room. He was startled to see a skeleton dressed in rotting clothes sitting in a chair at a desk.

Last night he had rolled beneath the bed so quickly that he hadn't even seen the skeleton. Harold noticed a bundle of yellow papers lying on the desk in front of it.

He picked up the papers, carried them to the window, and held them to the dawn's growing light. It was a kind of journal. Harold scanned the contents and was amazed.

The skeleton had been a man named John Benner. When Benner had died, he was sixty-five years old. At one time he had been a successful farmer. But when his wife died, he grew lonely—so lonely that he decided to create a companion.

Benner built it of cloth and hay and sticks. Made the mouth from the jawbone of a wolf. The rib cage he unearthed in one of his fields. He couldn't tell if the bones were human or animal. He'd never seen anything like them. He decided it was just the thing for his companion.

He even decided to give it a heart—one of the old valentine hearts his beloved wife had made him. He fastened the heart to the rib cage, closed up the chest with hay and sticks, dressed the scarecrow in his old evening clothes, and pinned an old stovepipe hat to its head. He kept the scarecrow in the house, placed it in chairs, set a plate before it at meal times, even talked to it.

And then one night it moved.

At first Benner was amazed and frightened, but in time he was delighted. Something about the combination of ingredients, the strange bones from the field, the wolf's jaw, the valentine heart, perhaps his own desires, had given it life.

The scarecrow never ate or slept, but it kept him company. It listened while he talked or read aloud. It sat with him at the supper table.

But come daylight, it ceased to move. It would find a place in the shadows—a dark corner or the inside of a cedar chest. There it would wait until the day faded and the night came.

In time, Benner became afraid. The scarecrow was a creature of the night, and it lost interest in his company. Once, when he asked it to sit down and listen to him read, it slapped the book from his hand and tossed him against the kitchen wall, knocking him unconscious.

A thing made of straw and bones, cloth and paper, Benner realized, was never meant to live, because it had no soul.

One day, while the scarecrow hid from daylight, Benner dragged it from its hiding place and pulled it outside. It began to writhe and fight him, but the scarecrow was too weak to do him damage. The sunlight made it smoke and crackle with flame.

Benner hauled it to the center of the field, raised it on a post, and secured it there by ramming a long staff through its chest and paper heart.

It ceased to twitch, smoke, or burn. The thing he created was now at rest. It was nothing more than a scarecrow.

The pages told Harold that even with the scarecrow controlled, Benner found he could not sleep at night. He let the farm go to ruin, became sad and miserable, even thought of freeing the scarecrow so that once again he might have a companion. But he didn't, and in time, sitting right here at his desk, perhaps after writing his journal, he died. Maybe of fear, or loneliness.

Astonished, Harold dropped the pages on the floor. The scarecrow had been imprisoned on that post for no telling how long. From the condition of the farm, and Benner's body, Harold decided it had most likely been years. *Then I came along,* he thought, *and removed the staff from its heart and freed it.*

Daylight, thought Harold. In daylight the scarecrow would have to give up. It would have to hide. It would be weak then.

Harold glanced out the window. The thin rays of morning were growing longer and redder, and through the trees he could see the red ball of the sun lifting over the horizon.

Less than five minutes from now he would be safe. A sense of comfort flooded over him. He was going to beat this thing. He leaned against the glass, watching the sunrise.

A pane fell from the window and crashed onto the roof outside.

Uh-oh, thought Harold, looking toward the door.

He waited. Nothing happened. There were no sounds. The scarecrow had not heard. Harold sighed and turned to look out the window again.

Suddenly, the door burst open and slammed against the wall. As Harold wheeled around, he saw a figure charging toward him, flapping its arms like the wings of a crow taking flight.

It pounced on him, smashed him against the window, breaking the remaining glass. Both went hurtling through the splintering window frame and fell onto the roof. They rolled together down the slope of the roof and onto the sandy ground.

It was a long drop—twelve feet or so. Harold fell on top of the scarecrow. It cushioned his fall, but he still landed hard enough to have the breath knocked out of him.

The scarecrow rolled him over, straddled him, pushed its hand tightly over Harold's face. The boy could smell the rotting hay and decaying sticks, feel the wooden fingers thrusting into his flesh. Its grip was growing tighter and tighter. He heard the scarecrow's wolf teeth snapping eagerly as it lowered its face to his.

Suddenly, there was a bone-chilling scream. At first Harold thought he was screaming, then he realized it was the scarecrow.

It leaped up and dashed away. Harold lifted his head for a look and saw a trail of smoke wisping around the corner of the house.

Harold found a heavy rock for a weapon, and forced himself to follow. The scarecrow was not in sight, but the side door of the house was partially open. Harold peeked through a window.

The scarecrow was violently flapping from one end of the room to the other, looking for shadows to hide in. But as the sun rose, its light melted the shadows away as fast as the scarecrow could find them.

Harold jerked the door open wide and let the sunlight in. He got a glimpse of the scarecrow as it snatched a thick curtain from a window, wrapped itself in it, and fell to the floor.

Harold spied a thick stick on the floor—it was the same one he had pulled from the scarecrow. He tossed aside the rock and picked up the stick. He used it to flip the curtain aside, exposing the thing to sunlight.

The scarecrow bellowed so loudly that Harold felt as if his bones and muscles would turn to jelly. It sprang from the floor, darted past him and out the door.

Feeling braver now that it was daylight and the scarecrow was weak, Harold chased after it. Ahead of him, the weeds in the field were parting and swishing like cards being shuffled. Floating above the weeds were thick twists of smoke.

Harold found the scarecrow on its knees, hugging its support post like a drowning man clinging to a floating log. Smoke coiled up from around the scarecrow's head and boiled out from under its coat sleeves and pant legs.

Harold poked the scarecrow with the stick. It fell on its back, and its arms flopped wide. Harold rammed the stick through its open chest, and through the valentine heart.

He lifted it from the ground easily with the stick. It weighed very little. He lifted it until its arms draped over the cross on the post. When it hung there, Harold made sure the stick was firmly through its chest and heart. Then he raced for his bike.

Sometimes even now, a year later, Harold thinks of his fishing gear and his camp shovel. But more often he thinks of the scarecrow. He wonders if it is still on its post. He wonders what would have happened if he had left it alone in the sunlight. Would that have been better? Would it have burned to ashes?

He wonders if another curious fisherman has been out there and removed the stick from its chest.

He hopes not.

He wonders if the scarecrow has a memory. It had tried to get Benner, but Benner had beat it, and Harold had beat it too. But what if someone else freed it and the scarecrow got him? Would it come after Harold too? Would it want to finish what it had started?

Was it possible, by some kind of supernatural instinct, for the scarecrow to track him down? Could it travel by night? Sleep in culverts and old barns and sheds, burying itself deep under dried leaves to hide from the sun?

Could it be coming closer to his home while he slept?

He often dreamed of it coming. In his dreams, Harold could see it gliding with the shadows, shuffling along, inching nearer and nearer

And what about those sounds he'd heard earlier tonight, outside his bedroom window? Were they really what he had concluded—dogs in the trash cans?

Had that shape he'd glimpsed at his window been the fleeting shadow of a flying owl, or had it been—Harold rose from bed, checked all the locks on the doors and windows, listened to the wind blow around the house, and decided not to go outside for a look.

THE GUEST

Eugen Bacon

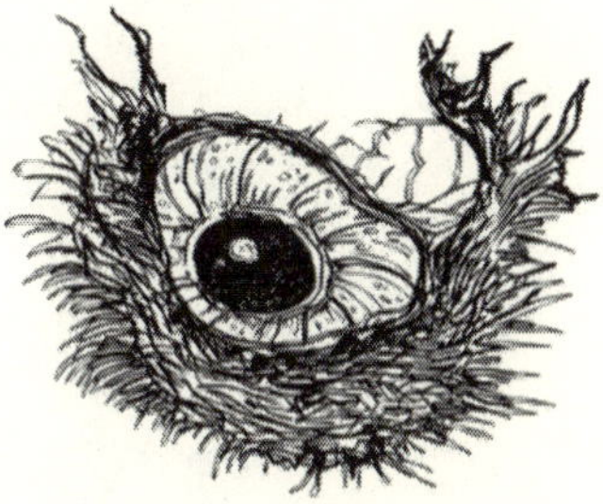

It started at a guesthouse. Muamadi was on the way home from work. *Pemba News* a complete thorn because the boss Kassam was on Muamadi's butt about breaking a new story—any story really. He was thinking about this when he saw the strangest thing. He nearly missed it, distracted as he was at first because a dry spell is not a good thing for a journalist. He had walked this way all the time, but had never seen something like this right on his path. There it stood: a colossal lump of stone jutting out of the ground in the middle of nowhere. It was as if he had stumbled into a dilapidated part of the universe. The road at his feet was all sand.

Then he saw that the stone was not a stone. It was a building with no windows. It was ugly as sin, right there on the deserted road.

Blink, and he saw the girl. She staggered his heart. How could he have missed her? She was leaning against a post on the baraza, the porch of the stone building. The whole structure now seemed to have blackened windows everywhere, story after story. It was short and it had height—how could a construction be both?

He eyed the girl.

She was radiant as a star, looked about twenty, hair a billow of curls. Wide, faraway eyes poured into him, and he felt like she was touching his soul. Something about her gaze made him think of all the beautiful things that had happened to him since he'd been a child. He remembered his mother's breath on his face. He remembered the touch of her fingers on his fat baby legs. He remembered her laughter, a sweet rolling chime that made him chuckle with glee. He'd forgotten it, that laughter, years since she died. He thought of a bite of wild honey maize—the favorite snack she made for him to munch like peanuts in a bowl.

Experiencing all this, he felt so happy he nearly cried.

The girl's eyes made him an offer and he said *yes*. He stepped closer, touched her hand. Her scent was a hint of anise—strong sweetness like the black licorice he once ate. He got the licorice from the Chief Nursing Office, a mzungu, the white nun, while covering a story of an outbreak of recurring typhoid when the flying doctors brought in another mzungu, a white pilot in a worsening ailment. He was crying hysterically, "Shetani! She bit me! She cursed me!" over and over.

"It's fleas, not a curse," Muamadi had said to the Chief Nursing Officer when he went to discuss a summary of the news he was going to cover about the hospital. "If he has a dog, they need to get rid of it."

"Maybe it's fleas," the CNO had said with somberness. "But it might not be a dog."

And she gave Muamadi licorice, perhaps to shut him up from nonsense.

The girl standing there, angled against a pillar, smelled like that licorice.

She wore a tiny frock shirt with a swishy skirt. He wanted to touch her pearl-jeweled neck peeking from a collar. He wanted to feel her arms the short elastic sleeves caressed, sleeves that were a fashion statement in themselves. He wanted to stroke her skin inside the thread-looped waist tie that was easy to untie. But the frock was partially buttoned and that would take some undoing until she was naked, he thought.

She parted her legs, and the ruffle skirt of the pink and olive frock shirt moved. Her bottle-shaped legs were perfect all the way up from red stilettos.

He forgot about the pilot and the dog. He forgot that he was a married man. That his wife Aisha was waiting for him at home with their toddler Issa at her breast.

The girl's skin was velvet cream. The sex that happened—

He was smoke and butter. His loins were full of the sweetest plums. Later, he remembered many times how she threw him on his back and straddled him. How she leaned forward with her weight and gripped his arms as she rode him. How the explosion shook him over and over and his buttocks flew to heaven and back.

Afterward, she reached for her purse, a clutch nano bag with a silver chain. Pulled out a cigarette. She handed him the lighter and he lit the cigarette for her, although he felt uncomfortable. The women in Zanzibar that he knew or didn't know—matter of fact any one he'd ever slept with—never smoked after sex. Never smoked at all, period.

She blew a swirl of smoke at his face. A waft filled with honey and cream, aged wood and spice touched his nostrils. It was a sweet aroma of vanilla and cinnamon, but it burned the back of his throat, made him cough as if it was crocodile pepper.

She smiled at his discomfiture. Still, she crushed the cigarette on the black oak bedhead. "Do you have a name?"

He told her. "And you?"

"Mgeni," she said.

"But it means a guest," he stammered. He thought his behind felt a bit tender.

"Then you're my guest. You can call me Suema."

He touched the beaded coil around her waist. "Is this a hirizi?"

"Yes," she said. "It's a protective charm."

"Protection from what?"

"From you, from me, from them."

"How so?"

"It's a charm that keeps me alive and human," she said.

He laughed at her joke. She laughed with him.

She tossed her head, studied him at an angle. "What do you do when you see a lion?" she asked.

"Play dead?"

"Mmhhh." She made to reach for another cigarette, changed her mind. "Tell me a good yarn."

So he told her about the mzungu at Pwani Hospital, the day the CNO gave him licorice. Muamadi was doing a hospital round, sniffing for stories. He told her about how the ambulance skidded with loud sirens outside Emergency. How paramedics rushed a white pilot on a stretcher. How the poor man was bent over in pain, crying in hysteria, "Shetani! She bit me! She cursed me!" over and over. How—as Muamadi watched—a furious rash continued spreading all over the man's torso.

"He had a fever that cooked him alive, you could see welts on his skin," Muamadi said, "and a cough of Abraham in his oldest age before an angel blessed him with a son. The nurses put him on a drip but he wasn't responding to any antibiotics. What he had was a resistant bug, they said. In the end, they flew him to Nairobi, but he died."

"And you thought it was fleas, not a curse?" she said.

This startled Muamadi. "How do you know?"

She looked at him, didn't say a thing and, somehow, he seemed to forget his question.

"You never know what kind of news a hospital spews at you," he heard himself saying in a voice that almost wasn't his. "This or that cancer. This or that head shaped like deformed barrels. This or that stoneman disease stiffening parts of a body in the most horrible way. I once saw a cauliflower face—warts all over, mold green and yellow."

"Is that the worst thing you ever saw?" she asked. Her wide faraway eyes felt easy, pushed words out of him.

"There was this bat man …"

"A bat man?" She sounded bemused.

"His skin was all furry," he said. "He had a snout on his face, all wrinkled and grooved. He sat on a bed at casualty, felt my stare and turned. He looked at me with such knowing, such pity as if I was the one in need, the one to be pitied. I rushed out of there."

Muamadi looked about the palatial room. It occurred to him that he didn't remember when he paid for the room at the lodgings, or how. He didn't have cash or a credit card. He didn't recollect who was at reception or if he signed a book. In his profession, signing a book was bad. It was leaving evidence, and he was a married man who felt solid about his wife. He didn't remember how he got into the regal bed with Suema. It seemed as if the moment their fingers touched, they were in a lush-carpeted room straining naked against each other.

He studied her. She would make a great story for *Pemba News*: a mystery woman on the island … Who was she? Why was she? He'd just need to untangle their connection.

"Who are you?" he asked.

"Perhaps you should be asking *what*, not who," she said.

"You're very secretive," he said.

"I let you find me. Now you owe me. I will collect."

"Oh?" He laughed.

She leaned and kissed him fully on the lips, and he felt dizzy.

Suddenly, he was stepping out of the baraza, fully dressed. He was back on the street and the stone building was gone. He found himself on his usual way home, a track across the busy market, people jostling past with their wares. Hawkers called out:

"Eh, ndizi!" The ripest baby bananas.

"Eh, viazi!" Freshly steamed sweet potatoes.

"Eh, machungwa!" A chilled crush of the freshest orange juice.

He could have thought the building and Suema and the delirious sex were all a dream, but something of its truth lingered on his mind.

That evening, out of guilt, he plucked a bunch of wild-growing flame lilies alongside the road. The brightest greenish-yellow leaves and crimson petals shaped like love hearts.

He walked home and found Issa squealing as if someone was cutting him. Aisha was rocking him this way, that way, giving him a tit, to no avail. Muamadi offered her the flowers.

"Do you want to kill me with that?" Aisha said. "There are other ways to kill me."

"Can't a man show love to his wife?" he said.

"Last time you showed me love, we wound up with a baby."

"Is that not a blessing?"

"It is, but not when a house is dry like ours." She looked at the flowers. "We can't eat these. Who needs flowers in a vase on a hungry stomach? What we need in this house are fresh eggs, unspoiled fish, new vegetables. We need more flour so I can cook you some chapati. We need to restock spices so I can make pilau again. And my milk is drying. Issa is crying all the time. Now you take him, it's your turn."

She threw the wailing bub into his arms.

"But—"

"Even your son is fishing in the rubbish bin for things to eat as he begins teething," she said. "I can't afford to buy him carrots."

She threw his gift of flowers into the bin.

He looked at the wastepaper basket he'd pilfered from work. The way Kassam rode his behind for a pittance, the stolen bin was nothing.

Issa screeched and reached back for his mother.

"Cling to him," Aisha said. "I need to pound what's left of the rice to make vitumbua so I can hawk them out in the street for the littlest money. Husband, you're becoming no good."

He didn't complain, because he knew that Aisha made the tastiest yeast pancakes with the most modest ingredients. He watched as she used a halved calabash to scoop rice from a nearly empty sack. She poured it into a pestle and pounded it, humming, with a mortar. Her melody calmed Issa, who stopped squirming and fell asleep on Muamadi's shoulder. He watched as she took a pinch of salt and yeast, tossed them into the mix, then added water. She took a wooden spoon and stirred the mixture into a wet texture ready for frying with a tiny spoonful of oil on a special heated pan—bottomed-out in moon curves to shape the vitumbua in the roundness and smallness of a child's fist.

Aisha was adept at cooking. She brushed each hole in the pan with oil, spooned in batter, and deftly flipped each pancake with a fork. The yeasty delights scooped out all glossy and golden brown, streaked with a charcoal garnish. The one Aisha let Muamadi taste was an oasis in a desert.

He watched fondly as she sat on a three-legged stool with a matted tray, calling out on the street in her confident hawker voice. "Eh, vitumbua!"

Sold the damn lot.

At bedtime, he grabbed his wife, yanked off her wraps and she said, "Oh?" then, "Ah!" Because he hadn't touched her since Issa was conceived. He fell between her legs and brushed his face on her leaking breasts. He moved to suck a nipple, but she pushed his head away. She clung to him as he angled his pelvis and wrapped her legs around his waist. He took her like a demon, yet there was no fury in their intercourse. They rocked gently together, nothing urgent, but the intensity of what they felt, how they felt—

"Oh, ah, ah!" they moaned softly in unison.

That night he dreamt he was swimming in the ocean. Something called out his name. "Muamadi! Muamadi!" He swam towards the sound, but the nearer he approached it, the further and further it got away from him. So he swam back ashore and stepped out of the water to find his body was full of sores.

Then he saw Issa, a little boy now, no longer a toddler. His son was rushing towards the humping waters. Muamadi waved at him to go back, go back.

"No! No! No!" he yelled at the boy.

But Issa threw himself with glee into a great big tide.

Muamadi rushed in after him, splashed about, coughed and splattered in his panic, but the boy was gone. The water had swallowed him completely without a trace.

He woke in a startle to the deepest silence, then a sound of slurping. To his horror, a small creature with a snout and the ears of a rat was on Aisha's chest. It was a gray bat, and it was sucking her milk. He slapped at it in fury, and it opened a pink mouth and bared white fangs. It wasn't milk, he now saw—the bat was sucking his wife's blood through her nipples. He slapped it again, shrieked at it, and it stretched its wings and flew out with its own screech. Strangely, none of all that noise woke Aisha, who was softly snoring.

But where was Issa?

He found the toddler on his back by the rubbish bin, hand clutching the flower stalk, a crush of red petals on his frothing mouth. Muamadi grabbed the floppy child with a cry, shook him. "Weye! Issa!" Shook him some more, nothing. "Issa, we!"

As he looked in horror, Aisha shuffled from the bedroom, moaning, "Uuuuuu, uuuuu." He saw the bulge on her stomach and realized she was not crying about Issa.

His wife was pregnant, and by the size of it—

How could Aisha possibly be *that* pregnant after one night? She looked as if labor was coming. And it was. "Uuuuuu, uuuuu."

A big splash on the floor told him her waters had broken. She fell to the ground, moaning and writhing in terrible agony. He remembered Suema and the hirizi around her waist. How she said it kept her alive and human. "Now you owe me," she had said. "I will collect." He was still thinking this as his wife exploded into a strew of body parts and blood.

He skreiched in horror at this violent death, then at the army of gray fleas that descended on the innards of his wife's scattering. The fleas were forming, reforming, as a single beast, shaping and reshaping itself. It now shuffled toward him, a blurry-headed beast whose snout became more visible as it neared. It had wings and a face all wrinkled and grooved.

He considered for a moment playing dead, as one might if it were a lion.

The house was suddenly a shroud and full of wailing. Sure, he'd cheated on his wife with a strange woman in a guesthouse, but was that a crime deserving of this fate? *What a headline it would make*, thought Muamadi, as the giant bat, a popo bawa, crawled toward him on all fours like a human. It left behind a trail of ashes and carted with it a stench of decay. The random spirit that preyed upon distracted men opened its mouth in a stretch, and Muamadi knew this was not a creature for which he could play dead.

THE LAST GHOST

Linda D. Addison

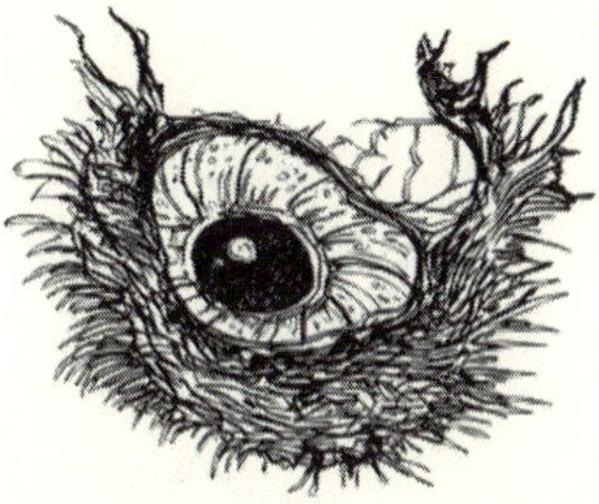

Fighting extinction
feeding off the distant echoes of life long gone,
she chased lost spirit animals
in the decaying remains of empty cities.

How dare they kill living creatures so efficiently,
leaving her the lone witness to
buildings, roads overgrown by witless plants,
inadequate participants in her afterlife commitment.

Her spectral ears desperate to invoke one scream,
one gasp of surprise, a raised eyebrow,
a glance of fear over the shoulder. Not to expire
again in this emptied planet.

And then they landed in a silver ship, not human, but
alive
nonetheless. Unrecognizable limbs and language,
but living creatures. So she waited and watched until
one was
dying, inhaled their fear to learn the language of
haunting anew.

The souls of those
that die suddenly
Weakened by
Light
Summoned/created by
"Calcu" or
"Kalku"
Feed milk + honey
to maintain

MILK, HONEY, AND BLOOD

Lucy Taylor

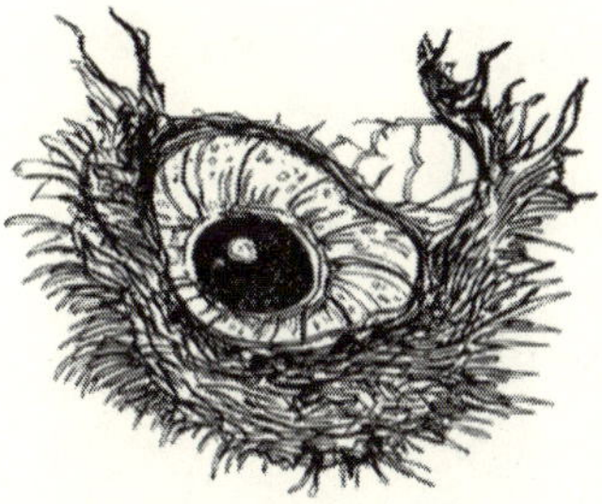

On the final week of our month-long trek through Patagonia, my brother Raine and I visited Dona Florencia, a stout, nut-brown elder from the Mapuche village where Raine taught English for a year after getting his degree in Cultural Anthropology. When I asked why Dona Florencia's *ruka,* a squat hut made of bamboo and woven grass, sat apart from the rest of the village, Raine told me the old woman was a witch, a *calcu*. She demanded privacy. To do what, he didn't say.

We sat on mud benches covered with sheepskin, eating ash-cooked tortilla bread and fire-roasted pinones. During the meal, we spoke English, but later, when Dona Florencia guided us down a path through the dense Chilean forest, she and Raine conversed only in the Mapuchen dialect, excluding me from the discussion. Soon we came to a three-foot-long hole scraped out of the moist dirt in a grove of ulmo trees. It was empty except for a few scraps of brightly colored fabric and the cracked plastic head of a doll.

I turned to my brother. "Was this a child's grave? What happened here?"

He ignored me and continued his intense conversation with the *calcu.* A strange word—*anchimayen*—was used several times by them both. My brother's tone made the word sound benign, but on Dona Florencia's lips, the four syllables cut the air like a curse. I was about to ask what it meant, but when Raine gave Dona Florencia an envelope thick with U.S. hundred-dollar bills, I was so shocked I left the question unasked.

I shouldn't have.

"With all that money did you buy a plot of land to build your own *ruka*?" I teased on the hike back to our rented hut.

He answered dead seriously. "Maybe one day, Kiara. For now, think of it as a down payment on good fortune."

"That much money must buy a shit load of good fortune."

A shit load of something, at least.

Before he began studying the Mapuchen culture, Raine hitchhiked around Mexico and Central and South America, exploring the edgier side of the supernatural in indigenous cultures. In Oaxaca, he told me a shaman took him night-flying on psylocibin. Smoking toad venom in the Peruvian jungle nearly killed him, he said, but also allowed him a glimpse of enlightenment. And in Haiti, he claimed to have witnessed a Bizango ceremony where a man who drank poison was brought back to life and another man was reduced to a zombie. His unquestioning willingness to explore the dark aspects of other cultures both frightened and intrigued me. I envied the casual, even reckless manner in which he threw himself into the unknown.

Envied him, at least, until I didn't.

Did I agree to trek the long, whip-thin length of Chile with him because I was sick of my humdrum job in marketing or bitter at the end of a relationship? Did I want a taste of the forbidden? Or, face it, did I just want to court an untimely death and I knew Raine was the way that I'd find it?

These were questions I asked myself later. On the trek back to our hut, however, I wasn't thinking about any of that; my sore back and blistered heel claimed all my attention. The strenuous hike sapped my energy. My last memory before falling asleep was of Raine standing outside on the deck overlooking the forest and lake, scanning the trees with binoculars.

Then suddenly hours must have passed, and he was shaking me awake. "Kiara, come outside!"

I pulled on my boots and followed him out the squeaky sliding door onto the deck.

"Look!"

Above us, the stars pinwheeled in a glittering gyroscope. I made out the Southern Cross and Centaurus, familiar waypoints in the Southern Hemisphere. Then I saw something uncanny, out of place in this gorgeous, but normally well-ordered universe. Above the treetops, a luminous globe jittered and bounced, shedding shards of blue flame before dipping out of sight, then reappearing.

Raine handed me a flashlight. "Hurry!"

We descended the stairs and plunged into the forest, following the blue fireball that seemed to pulse like an alien heart, luring us on.

"What the hell is that?"

He whispered, "Quiet. If you make noise, it may get angry."

It? My mind swirled with images of the pumas that prowled

these dark forests, the wild boars with their fearsome tusks that could mangle and gut.

Raine marched ahead. For a few minutes, we wove through the trees, our crisscrossing beams illuminating cypress and beech, the towering coihue trees and stately pinoneros. Something exploded out of the bushes a few feet away. I yelped with fright, but it was only a pair of armadillos, grub-hunting little eyes gleaming as they slithered through the beam of my flashlight.

We'd lost sight of the blue globe. Raine muttered a curse and walked faster. I was following him, when a low, mewling cry breeched the silence, the whimper of an injured animal or a child in distress. I froze. The sound came again, sharper now, rife with urgency. Forgetting Raine, I moved toward it. My light swept over clumps of underbrush, past saplings and towering stands of bamboo. I made out a mass of thick, matted vines that resembled a bed of green pythons. In the center of this tangle crouched a child no more than two or three years old, swaddled in filthy-looking rags. The blue light flickered around her.

I heard Raine hiss, "Kiara, don't move!" but I was already running, obeying an instinct as old as the caves to come to the aid of a child in danger. I reached to scoop her up in my arms, then recoiled with a gasp. My flashlight illuminated a flat, deformed face, coin-slit eyes in an over-large head, a mouth toothy and crude as that of a badly carved pumpkin.

Raine yelled my name. As I began to turn toward him, the blue fire blazed wildly, then exploded. Shards perforated my eyes and scalded my skin. I blacked out and found myself soaring through a terrible dream: a little girl exhumed from her grave and Dona Florencia, under a huge ulmo tree, sheering off the limbs and head of the corpse, stitching them into a demonic facsimile of a child. I heard men chanting and the low brassy notes of a *trutrunka* as Dona Florencia imbued the terrible fetish with ungodly life. Raine assisted her. The ulmo tree shivered loose a deluge of coins.

When the coins became leaves pelting my face, I woke up on the ground, cocooned in a caul of blackness. Stars, moon, the earth itself, all had vanished, gobbled down by this infernal dark. It was the sound of Raine's moans that made me fight through the brain fog and try to stand, but I was too weak and dizzy to walk. I crawled toward his voice and found him on the ground, flailing wildly at that insatiable sky.

When I spoke to him, terror contorted his once-handsome face.

"Kiara, help me! I'm blind!"

How we got back to the hut I barely remember, only that Raine stumbled along behind me with his hands on my shoulders. Sometimes his weight made my knees buckle and I begged him to loosen his grip. He complied, but a few minutes later, he was again pressing me into the dirt. When what I thought was a quartet of cypress trees morphed into support beams for the deck of the hut, I shed tears of relief.

Inside I rinsed out the swollen slits where Raine's green eyes used to be, but it caused so much pain he grew furious and swatted my hands away. "Jesus, Kiara, this was your fault! You frightened the anchimayen!"

"I thought it was a child!"

He punched the arm of the chair so hard the wood cracked. "You didn't listen! Your stupidity brought this on us!"

We sat in silence then, a blind man quietly crying, and his terrified sister, while the night grew colder and the merciless stars resumed their right place in the heavens. Raine put his head in his hands. Finally he looked up and started to talk.

"The Mapuche sorcerers have known about the anchimayen since the beginning of time. When a child dies, sometimes the body disappears. The relatives know what the body's being used for, but they're afraid to say anything. They know, for good or for evil, the anchimayen will always serve the calcu who brought it into being."

"Or whoever the calcu sold it to," I muttered.

The depth of this depravity seemed to elude Raine, because he only shrugged and went on, "The anchimayens have protected the Mapuche from their enemies for centuries. Just the sight of the sky filling with balls of blue flame sent the Spanish invaders running for their lives."

"And the girl in the grave, did Dona Florencia kill her? Or did you?"

Raine's jaw clenched so tight I thought the bone might pop through, and I leaned away from him, some primitive part of me suddenly on high alert. I knew my brother had a volatile temper, but this was the first time I felt like he was approaching a dangerous tipping point.

He swallowed and exhaled violently, as though ridding himself of some poison. For now, the moment of danger had passed. "Neither of us touched her. She died of fever, as children here sometimes do."

"A desecrated grave, a mutilated corpse, what's the harm, right?"

To my surprise, instead of raging, he spoke with reverence, like a man extolling a lover. "The anchimayen is a miracle, don't you see? Its very existence proves what I've always believed—that our existence is more than a meaningless joke with humans as pawns. The undead move among us. They observe us, teach us, sometimes they punish us. An anchimayen can be dangerous, but the one who owns it has unimaginable power."

Which you've always wanted, I thought.

My disgust at the shameless way he coveted this horror made me fall silent, which played on Raine's nerves. Soon he was calling out for me. "Kiara? Are you still there?"

I wanted to ignore him, but when I looked into his ruined eyes, the grief I felt was almost as intense as if he had died. "I'm still here."

I did something then that surprised us both. Impulsively I took his hand and kissed the back of it, where the thick veins bulged. We did this as children, when the adults thought it was funny and sweet, and then after we got older, when they found it less so. I hadn't kissed my brother's hand in a very long time. He seemed comforted by it.

"Sleep now." I said. "We'll both feel better tomorrow. Your sight will come back."

I spoke these things as though I knew.

I didn't.

I woke to an orange dawn streaming through the shutters and the sight of the anchimayen crouched like a malicious doll at the foot of Raine's cot. Its black, slitted eyes, like those of a sadistic child, regarded me with a disquieting hunger. I could see the stitches where its arms had been sewn on with black thread, but carelessly, leaving gaps where the bone showed through. Or perhaps that had been the intent—the exposed bone made its appearance all the more ghastly. When I got up, it flashed razorblade teeth, and an infantile squeal spilled from its pursed mouth like drool.

Raine sat up, nostrils twitching.

"It's here," I said, although I realized he already knew. The damp reek of grave dirt and decomposition permeated the room.

The anchimayen hopped to the floor and toddled toward me, clumsily at first as though mimicking a living child before it gave up the game and began to racing around me, flashing its small, vicious teeth. I felt a surge of panic. "Raine? Make it stop! I think it's going to hurt me!"

"Stop it," he said lazily, as though nothing of great importance was at stake. The anchimayen backed away with teeth still bared.

Raine held me until I stopped shaking. "I need you to do something for me, Kiara. The anchimayen requires certain foods. You must go back to see Dona Florencia and tell her to give you what it needs."

"And leave you alone?"

"Don't worry about me. Just do it. And be quick about it, okay?" He said this as casually as if he were asking me to run to the store for beer.

"But that will take a whole day. We need to leave now!"

"After we feed the anchimayen. Understand me, this is not negotiable."

"You need a doctor."

"Obviously. Which is why you should hurry. When you come back, then we can decide what we want to do."

Across the room by the slider, I heard the anchimayen's toenails scraping wood and the low hiss of blue fire seething under its dead skin. At that moment, trekking back to Dona Florencia's village seemed infinitely better than remaining here with Raine and the undead abomination by the door.

In the drawer of kitchen implements I chose the deadliest

looking knife I could find and wrapped Raine's hand around the hilt.

"Keep this close. Just in case it stops obeying you."

"You don't understand. It belongs to me now." His free hand found its way into my hair. "Everything here belongs to me."

I jerked away from him.

"Oh, now you're angry?" His voice got hard and mean. "Do you even remember the trail we used yesterday? Or will you get lost and wander in circles? Can you even find your way to Dona Florencia?"

His contempt was infuriating. "Watch me."

I realized what I'd said at the same moment Raine did. Absurdly, insanely, we both burst into hysterical laughter.

"If you've come for another anchimayen, you've wasted your time," snapped Dona Florencia. "Just the one child died recently. Now only useless old people fill the graves."

Her aged fingers spidered over a loom, creating a vivid red and green rug. Between us crackled a fire surrounded by volcanic stones. When I first entered her ruka, she'd berated me in both English and Mapuchen, but finally calmed down enough to resume her weaving. I couldn't fault her for being angry—I'd barged into her home without announcement or invitation. When I told her the anchimayen had blinded Raine, she was unmoved.

"What did he expect? It has power, the anchimayen. Only a fool tries to hunt it down like a wild pig."

I spoke without thinking. "So why create such a monstrosity?"

"Your brother was the one who summoned it. I just sewed together the parts."

In my fear-addled brain, the scrape and rattle of the loom sounded like the anchimayen's long, clicking nails. I thought of the empty grave and suppressed a fierce urge to pick up one of the stones and smash in the hag's head.

"Dona Florencia, we need your help. If you could give me food for the anchimayen"—I decided to push my luck—"and medicine for Raine's eyes, then I'll be on my way."

"For his eyes, Raine has the anchimayen. It will guard him night and day and kill his enemies."

"My brother doesn't want that."

"Maybe you don't know what he wants."

With that, she creaked to her feet and left me alone in the ruka. I grew nervous waiting, but eventually she returned with a frightened-looking young boy struggling to carry a large, stoppered clay jug. He set it next to me, bowed to Dona Florencia, and scurried away.

"Goat's milk and honey," she said. "Use it carefully, because I won't give you more. Remember the anchimayen's weakness is greed. Feed it too much and it will eat itself into a stupor and sleep for days. And if you want to make it completely loyal, add blood to the mix." I started to ask if goat's blood would do, but the casual cruelty in her burning black eyes kept me silent.

I muscled the jug into my pack.

Blood, I thought. *Never.*

To my relief, the anchimayen was nowhere in sight when I returned, so I locked the sliding door behind me. Foolish to think a sheet of glass could keep out hell's imp, but I had to try. Raine was sleeping, the knife next to him. I set the jug on the table and began to pack our things. Just the essentials, enough to get us to the nearest town. I wanted to be on the trail, headed away from this accursed place at first light.

Suddenly Raine spoke up so clearly I knew he'd been feigning sleep all along. "Sister? Did you get the food?"

"I did."

"Why are you zipping up the knapsacks?"

"Because we're leaving tomorrow. We'll follow the lake south until we get to a town. I'll tie a rope to my belt for you to hold onto. We'll go slowly. I'll help you."

"I don't need your help." He stood up abruptly, spreading his arms wide in what would have looked like celebration except for the knife in his hand. "Now I can see!"

"Your sight has come back?" For a wondrous instant, I believed him. But when I looked into his glazed-over eyes, they were empty as eggs. I raised one hand and a forefinger. "If you can see, tell me how many fingers I'm holding up."

"I meant Inner Sight. The portal into the Divine Chaos. Where the anchimayens roam before a calcu sews together their new bodies. My blindness is a gift, I understand that now. I see our kind's damnation and how beings from the other realms guide us along the path to extinction." He raised the knife, twisting it back and forth. "Don't worry, Kiara, we still have some time left. A few years at least so I can learn from Dona Florencia how to bring forth undead creatures myself."

My eyes were focused on the knife, the way the sunlight kissed the blade as if it were holy relic. In Raine's mind, perhaps it was. "I'm not staying here. If you don't come with me, I'll go alone."

He came closer.

"Please, Raine, you don't need the knife."

"I disagree. I trusted you enough to show you the miracle of the anchimayen. I believed your eyes could be opened, too, but I was wrong."

"Raine, no."

He halted. "Oh, don't be silly, Kiara. You think I'd hurt you? I wouldn't do that, would I?" I heard the clicking-scraping sound above me and looked up. The anchimayen leered down from the rafters.

"Kill her!" Raine said.

I never saw the creature jump down, but suddenly it was on the table next to me, inches from the jug of milk and honey. I prayed the sweet smell would distract it, but its focus was entirely on me; the tiny, razor-edged teeth gnashed for me alone. I bolted for the door, but the anchimayen got there first, its over-sized head bobbing gleefully, wide mouth puckered in a smirk. It pursued me at a lazy stalk until it had me trapped behind the table. I begged Raine to call it off. I promised I'd live with him and care for him. I promised anything. Finally he held up a hand. "Stop."

I sagged with relief until he said, "I'll kill her. It's my duty!"

The anchimayen kept me cornered behind the table while Raine inched forward with the knife. I tried to slip past him, but each time, the anchimayen blocked my way, assisting its insane master. "I see you, sister, in my visions," Raine singsonged. "I smell your skin, your hair, your cunt. I always know where you are."

The knife slashed the air inches from my eyes. Next time he wouldn't miss. I grabbed the jug and shouted, "Here I am, brother" and when he lunged at me, I slammed the heavy pot full in his face. I heard cartilage crunch and saw a crimson tooth spin across the room. Blood fountained from his pancaked nose. The jug hit the floor and smashed open as Raine dropped like a stone, milk and honey gushing over his ruined face. Dona Florencia was right. There is no greed like that of an anchimayen. Whatever loyalty the creature had to Raine was no match for its appetite. It gobbled down the sweet red feast while the still-living meat thrashed and bellowed.

The screams pursued me down the stairs and deep into the forest. My name on Raine's lacerated lips throbbed inside my ears. His unholy shrieks lasted far longer than his life.

Even now, days later, in my room at a backwater flophouse in this small coastal town, I can still hear his horrible dying.

The anchimayen showed up yesterday. With dried blood on its bloated cheeks and a lusty hunger in its eyes. It sat on my belly and watched me sleep, and when I tried to explore this decrepit town, it became a blue globe hovering above my head, always visible to me, but unseen by the tourists and trinket sellers, the venders of churros and hawkers of tokens to ward off evil spells.

This morning I knew what I had to do.

The milk and honey were easy enough to find in a small grocery. The knife I finagled from an Aussie trekker looks wicked sharp.

Now the anchimayen fixes its dead stare on me as I huddle in the corner. Its hunger grows and my terror mounts.

I hold the knife blade against my thigh and then across my wrist.

It's just a matter of where I cut first.

GOLD IS GOD

(gāoguài—strange ghosts)

Ai Jiang

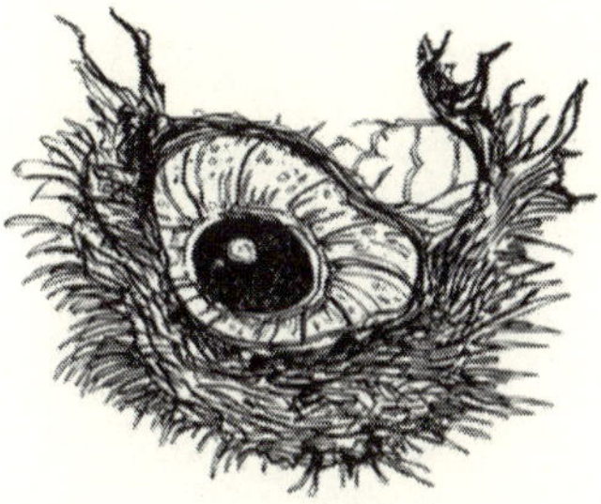

this is a dissonance for dead
darlings, one taught by those
who say gold is god, that survival
requires gold, that belonging
requires gold, that attraction
requires gold, that without—

but you desired not gold but
something to quell loneliness
left by parents left, and each
minute they spent not on you
they offer a grain of gold that
collects like falling sand of hour
glasses until what remains
are two halves both full, with
sand with nowhere to fall but

why does full feel foul—empty?

you, with nowhere to go, you,
with no one to turn to, but gold,
like sunlight, like warmth, yet
it is neither, it is cold metal,
held in your hands, and it is—

expensive, extravagant, eternal
surviving through time, through
economic collapse, through the fall
of dynasties, the destruction
of empires, the demolition
of civilizations.

And yet—
And yet—
And yet—
Have you
survived?

As the living reach towards
you with greed brighter than
emeralds, desire foaming from
their lips, dripping like acid against
your skin, you know they will die,
like you, and will return,
like you, become gold like god,
like you, because gold is god,
like—

ABOUT THE AUTHORS

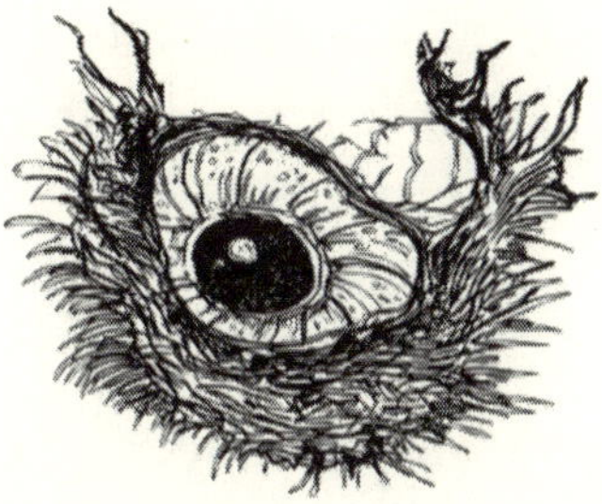

Linda D. Addison is an award-winning author of five collections, including *How To Recognize A Demon Has Become Your Friend.* She has been honored with the HWA Lifetime Achievement Award, HWA Mentor of the Year and SFPA Grand Master of Fantastic Poetry. She is a member of CITH, HWA, SFWA, SFPA and IAMTW. Find her in anthologies: *Blood Games: A Vampire Anthology*, *Playlist of the Damned, Weird Tales: 100 Years of Weird, Enter Boogeyman, Folk Horror,* and *Bestiary of Blood: Modern Fables & Dark Tales*, including upcoming *Everything Endless*, a poetry collaboration with Jamal Hodge.

Her site: www.lindaaddisonwriter.com.

Eugen Bacon is an African Australian author. She's a British Fantasy and Foreword Indies Award winner, a twice World Fantasy Award finalist, and a finalist in other awards, including the Shirley Jackson, Philip K. Dick Award, as well as the Nommo Awards for speculative fiction by Africans. Eugen was announced in the honor list of the Otherwise Fellowships for "doing exciting work in gender and speculative fiction". *Danged Black Thing* made the Otherwise Award Honor List as a "sharp collection of Afro-Surrealist work". Visit her at www.eugenbacon.com.

Ramsey Campbell is a British writer considered by a number of critics to be one of the great masters of horror fiction. T. E. D. Klein has written that "Campbell reigns supreme in the field today," while S. T. Joshi has said that "future generations will regard him as the leading horror writer of our generation, every bit the equal of Lovecraft or Blackwood."

In addition to writing numerous international bestsellers, genre defining novels, and receiving nearly universal acclaim, he has also been a vocal defender of the written word and its enduring importance.

Stephanie Ellis writes dark speculative prose and poetry, and is based in Wrexham, UK. Her novels include *The Five Turns of the Wheel, Reborn, The Woodcutter*, and *The Barricade* as well as the novellas, *Bottled* and *Paused.* Her short stories appear in the collections *The Reckoning* and *Devil Kin* as well as a variety of anthologies and magazines. She is a Rhysling and Elgin Award nominated poet and has written the collection *Foundlings* (with Cindy O'Quinn), *Lilith Rising* and *Mason Gorey: A Haunting Catskill Elegy* (with Shane Douglas Keene), and *Metallurgy*, as well as appearing in the *HWA Poetry Showcase*. She can be found at https://stephanieellis.org.

Maxwell I. Gold is a multiple award nominated author who writes prose poetry and short stories in weird and cosmic fiction. His work has appeared in numerous anthologies and magazines including

Weirdbook Magazine, Space and Time Magazine, Startling Stories, Strange Horizons, *Tales from OmniPark* Anthology, *Shadow Atlas: Dark Landscapes of the Americas* and more. He's the author of Oblivion in Flux: A Collection of Cyber Prose from Crystal Lake Publishing.

Maxwell's books include a collaborative book of poems titled *Möbius Lyrics* with Bram Stoker Award winner Angela Yuriko Smith; Bram Stoker Award nominated poetry collection, *Bleeding Rainbows and Other Broken Spectrums* from Hex Publishers and an *Other Mythology* prose poetry chapbook from Interstellar Flight Press.

He lives in Ohio with two dogs Marshall and Otto, and currently serves as the Executive Director for the Horror Writers Association.

Ai Jiang is a Chinese-Canadian writer, Ignyte, Bram Stoker, and Nebula Award winner, and Hugo, Astounding, Locus, Aurora, and BFSA Award finalist from Changle, Fujian currently residing in Toronto, Ontario. Her work can be found *in F&SF, The Dark, The Masters Review*, among others. She is the recipient of Odyssey Workshop's 2022 Fresh Voices Scholarship and the author of *Linghun* and *I AM AI.* The first book of her novella duology, *A Palace Near the Wind*, is forthcoming 2025 with Titan Books. Find her on X (@AiJiang_), Instagram (@ai.jian.g), and online (http://aijiang.ca).

Gwendolyn Kiste is the three-time Bram Stoker Award-winning author of The Rust Maidens, Reluctant Immortals, And Her Smile Will Untether the Universe, Pretty Marys All in a Row, The Invention of Ghosts, and Boneset & Feathers. Her short fiction and nonfiction have appeared in outlets including Lit Hub, Nightmare, Tor Nightfire, Titan Books, Vastarien, Best American Science Fiction and Fantasy, and The Dark among others. She's a Lambda

Literary Award winner, and her fiction has also received the This Is Horror award for Novel of the Year as well as nominations for the Premios Kelvin and Ignotus awards.

Originally from Ohio, she now resides on an abandoned horse farm outside of Pittsburgh with her husband, their calico cat, and not nearly enough ghosts.

Joe R. Lansdale is the author of fifty novels and four hundred shorter works, including stories, essays, reviews, film and TV scripts, introductions and magazine articles, as well as a book of poetry. His work has been made into films, animation, comics, and he has won numerous awards including the Edgar, Raymond Chandler Lifetime Award, numerous Bram Stoker Awards, and the Spur Award.

His work has been made into films, among them *Bubba Hotep, Cold in July*, as well as the acclaimed TV show, *Hap and Leonard.* His novel *The Thicket* is currently filming. He has also had works adapted to *Masters of Horror* on Showtime, Netflix's *Love, Death & Robots*, and Shudder's *Creepshow*. He has written scripts for *Batman the Animated Series*, and other animation.

He has received numerous awards and recognition for horror, crime, historical fiction, as well as others. He lives in Nacogdoches with his wife Karen and pit bull, RooRoo.

Tim Lebbon is a New York Times-bestselling horror, thriller and fantasy writer from a little village in South Wales. He's written over 45 novels, including some in established universes such as Star Wars, Alien, Predator, Hellboy, and Firefly. He has won a World Fantasy Award, four British Fantasy Awards, a Bram Stoker Award, a Scribe Award and a Dragon Award. Tim has also worked on the major new computer game 'Resurgence', and he's written audio drama for Audible.

His novel THE SILENCE is a Netflix movie starring Kiernan Shipka and Stanley Tucci. His novella PAY THE GHOST is a Halloween movie starring Nicolas Cage. He is currently developing several other projects for the screen.

As well as reading and writing he loves running, biking and swimming, and often puts them all together in long-distance triathlons. He raced six Ironmans so far, and has no plans to stop just yet.

Thersa Matsuura is an author and podcaster who has been living in Japan for thirty plus years. She's a graduate of the Clarion West (2015) workshop, a recipient of the HWA's Mary Wollstonecraft Shelley Scholarship (2015), and the author of two short story collections, *A Robe of Feathers and Other Stories* (Counterpoint Press LLC) and *The Carp-Faced Boy and Other Tales* (Independent Legions Press). The latter of which was nominated for a Bram Stoker Award (2017). Her upcoming book (*The Book of Japanese Folklore*) will be published by Adams Media in spring of 2024. She's also had many stories published in magazines, anthologies, and serialized in the Asahi English Newspaper.

Thersa shares the more obscure, strange, and fascinating bits of her research and experiences on her podcast, *Uncanny Japan*.

Ben Monroe has spent most of his life in Northern California, wher he lives in the East Bay Area with his wife and two children. He is the author of *In the Belly of the Beast and Other Tales of Cthulhu Wars*, *The Seething*, the graphic novel *Planet Apocalypse*, and short stories in several anthologies.

You can find more information about him and his work at www.benmonroe.com

Lisa Morton is a screenwriter, author of non-fiction books, and prose writer whose work was described by the American Library Association's Readers' Advisory Guide to Horror as "consistently dark, unsettling, and frightening." She is a six-time winner of the Bram Stoker Award®, the author of four novels and 200 short stories, and a world-class Halloween and paranormal expert. Her recent releases include the novella *Placerita* (co-written with John Palisano) and the Rondo Hatton Award-winning *The Art of the Zombie Movie*. She also hosts the popular weekly *Ghost Report* podcast. Lisa lives in Los Angeles and online at www.lisamorton.com.

Cindy O'Quinn is a Bram Stoker Award®-winning writer. Her poetry has been nominated for the Elgin, Rhysling, and Dwarf Star Awards. She lives in the beautiful mountains of West Virginia, which make an ideal backdrop for writing.

Lucy Taylor's fiction has appeared in the anthologies *Peel Back the Skin, Body Shock, Pain Freak, The Big Book of Blasphemy, Cutting Edge, The Best of the Best Horror of the Year*, and many more. Her longer works include the horror/western *Desolation*, the Stoker-finalist novelette *Sweetlings*, the novels *Dancing With Demons, Spree, Eternal Hearts, Saving Souls*, and the Stoker Award-winning *The Safety of Unknown Cities*. Her fiction has been translated into Italian, Spanish, German, French, Russian, and Czech. Most recently, Taylor's work can be found in the anthologies *Erotic Horror for Horny Housewives* and *Enter Boogeyman*.

Taylor lives in the high desert outside Santa Fe, New Mexico.

David Wellington, aka D. Nolan Clark, aka David Chandler is the author of over twenty novels of action, horror, suspense, and drama, including the *Monster Island* trilogy, the *Den of Thieves* trilogy, the

Jim Chapel trilogy spy thrillers, and *Positive*, his grand zombie opus. His space horror novel, *The Last Astronaut*, was shortlisted for the Arthur C Clark award. Most recently, he published *Paradise-1*, which received a starred review in Publishers Weekly. He has also worked with comic books, video games, and been published in numerous anthologies

You can find more information about him and his work at www.davidwellington.net

F Paul Wilson has received widespread acclaim, countless awards in multiple genres and has been published in over 20 languages. He has published over 50 books including the international best seller and genre-defining novel *The Keep*, featured in over 100 anthologies, and has written for Disney Interactive and the Sci-Fi Channel among others. Additionally, he is a part-time practicing family physician.

Stephanie M. Wytovich is an American poet, novelist, and essayist. She is a recipient of the Bram Stoker Award, the Elizabeth Matchett Stover Memorial Award, the 2021 Ladies of Horror Fiction Writers Grant, and has received the Rocky Wood Memorial Scholarship for non-fiction writing. Wytovich is a member of the Science Fiction Poetry Association, an active member of the Horror Writers Association, and a graduate of Seton Hill University's MFA program for Writing Popular Fiction. Follow her at www.stephaniemwytovich.com and on Twitter and Instagram @SWytovich and @thehauntedbookshelf. You can also sign up for her newsletter at https://stephaniemwytovich.substack.com/.

About the Editors

Stephanie Ellis writes dark speculative prose and poetry, and is based in Wrexham, UK. Her novels include *The Five Turns of the*

Wheel, Reborn, The Woodcutter, and *The Barricade* as well as the novellas, *Bottled* and *Paused.* Her short stories appear in the collections *The Reckoning* and *Devil Kin* as well as a variety of anthologies and magazines. She is a Rhysling and Elgin Award nominated poet and has written the collection *Foundlings* (with Cindy O'Quinn), *Lilith Rising* and *Mason Gorey: A Haunting Catskill Elegy* (with Shane Douglas Keene), and *Metallurgy*, as well as appearing in the *HWA Poetry Showcase*. She can be found at https://stephanieellis.org.

Noel Osualdini is an Australian writer, consultant editor and proofreader who has worked on numerous speculative fiction and young adult titles. Some of his own horror stories, published originally in anthologies and e-zines, were collected in *Train Wreck and Other Stories* (2018). *Stingers,* his recent collection with German author T.M.McLean, was shortlisted for the collections category of the 2023 Australian Shadows Award. He lives southeast of Melbourne with his partner Joanne and their family.

Made in the USA
Middletown, DE
11 May 2025

75217443R00135